I0822722

BALTIMORE

Baltimore

English translation by Persida Bošković

Front cover and layout design by Sadie Crofts

Serbian Modern Literature Series (SMiLeS)
Published by:
Blooming Twig Books
New York / Tulsa
www.bloomingtwig.com

Hardcover: ISBN 978-1-61343-052-1
Paperback: ISBN 978-1-61343-053-8
eBook: ISBN 978-1-61343-054-5

Printed in the United States by arrangement with
Geopoetika publishing (Belgrade, Serbia)
www.geopoetika.com

BALTIMORE

JELENA LENGOLD

TRANSLATED FROM THE SERBIAN
BY PERSIDA BŎSKOVÍC

PUBLISHED BY BLOOMING TWIG BOOKS
NEW YORK / TULSA
2014

BALTIMORE

THIS CIRCUS IS FALLING DOWN ON ITS KNEES
THE BIG TOP IS CRUMBLING DOWN
IT'S RAINING IN BALTIMORE FIFTY MILES EAST
WHERE YOU SHOULD BE, NO ONE'S AROUND

I NEED A PHONE CALL
I NEED A RAINCOAT
I NEED A BIG LOVE

I NEED A PHONE CALL

FROM THE SONG "RAINING IN BALTIMORE"

BY COUNTING CROWS

ONE

Let's get something clear first:

If this is going to be one of those stories in which everyone is nice and polite, then we'd better stop now.

I would like to tell you everything about everything, and there is so much to say. You get that, don't you? When you want to say it all, not everyone can be pleasant and polite. Least of all me.

Then, there's my family. With its highly developed sense of drama, a trait I too acquired at an early age as its equal member.

Then all those diseases, which frightened me and still do.

The numerous lies I sometimes lose track of and then think I'll get confused and forget what I said and to whom.

The amount of disdain I feel, mostly in the morning, while I'm taking off my nightgown, throwing it on the washing machine and getting into the bathtub.

The things I try to forget, but sometimes go back to, then chase away yet again and remember once more… this can be exhausting, you know.

The predictability of certain conversations – well, this is perhaps the worst of all.

The predictability of everything that follows.

And immediately after, or parallel to this, the hope that soon someone will surprise me in a superior and completely magical way. But, this doesn't happen anymore. If it ever did. All right, it used to happen, but back then I was more easily surprised.

When do we stop being young? When we feel back pain for the first time, or when there is nothing left to surprise us?

TWO

The time difference between Belgrade and Baltimore is six hours.

You might think this is crazy, but almost every day at 2:15 p.m., I sit at my computer and watch this guy in Baltimore on his way to work. He has the misfortune of living on a corner where one of those street cameras was installed. This is the location of a fast-food place. A street light. A bus stop. Nothing out of the ordinary.

He leaves his building every morning at 8:15 a.m., local time, usually carrying a briefcase. Naturally, I gave him a name. It's Edgar. Along with a name, I also gave him a biography. Edgar works for an insurance company.

He's single. That is to say, I've never seen him leave his apartment in the morning with a hottie. It looks like he doesn't have a dog either. He walks out of his building and waits for the bus, completely unaware of the fact that some silly woman from Belgrade is watching him as he goes to work.

I wait for the bus with him almost every day. The angle at which the camera was set up enables me to always see only a part of his face, and sometimes Edgar turns his back to me as he looks to see if his bus is coming.

Sometimes Edgar is late. He runs out of his building with a sandwich in his hand.

Sometimes he walks slowly, looking tired, as if he hadn't slept all night.

Sometimes he stares at some papers, without even looking up, while walking down the path from his building to the bus stop. As he waits for the bus, he continues his reading.

Always alone. He never carries an umbrella. If it does rain, Edgar just pulls his hood over his head and shelters that briefcase of his under his jacket. This brought me to the conclusion that the content of the briefcase was more important to Edgar than his own head.

By this time, my work day has long begun and I usually

imagine myself buying an overseas plane ticket some day and then flying to Baltimore, getting out of the airplane and into a yellow cab, giving the cab driver the name of that street, arriving at the bus stop at precisely 8:10 a.m., local time, and waiting for Edgar to appear. He arrives wearing his yellowish hooded jacket. I look at him and say:

"Hello, Edgar. I know everything about you and your life. I know how lonely you are. Fuck going to work today because I've travelled halfway across the world to spend this day with you. Let's go to the zoo. Let's go to a big park. Tell me what it's like in this insurance company, Edgar. Are they giving you a hard time?"

This is usually when my inspiration gives out on me.

Edgar, whose name of course isn't Edgar at all, would probably see me as just another crazy woman with a strange accent, move back a step in a politically correct manner, and turn away from me.

Or, he just might surprise me. Who knows?

I made an effort to be on time. Even though I knew this could also be construed to mean something. Everything could be construed to mean something. If you're late. If you forget an appointment. If you arrive early. All these things can give you away. All right, then. I'll try to be punctual, regardless of what it might reveal about me.

I pressed the button on the intercom at precisely a minute to six.

She opens the door and tells me to wait in the front room. I guess that means the previous patient is still with her. Then she disappears again, somewhere in the back.

Not very professional, I think to myself. Why is it that I can't be late while she can keep me waiting, and for our first appointment no less?

Maybe this is some sort of tactic? Maybe there's a small camera, over there above the sink, which records what the patient is doing while waiting to go in for his psychotherapy? Maybe she left her purse here intentionally, along with her notepad containing who knows what sort of information, and a computer? How could she possibly think I would be so naïve?

Okay, looking over the room. Even if the camera was taping me, looking around is normal. I don't suppose she expects me to sit here and stare into one spot? Not very imaginative posters. Emphasis on the "female" touch. Dried flowers. Aquarelles portraying romantic pregnant women. Numerous real potted plants. Yuck.

I have a clear view of a wall clock from the bench where I'm sitting. Ten after six. This is now becoming a bit rude, don't you think?

I can hear someone laughing in the other room. If only they were crying, then delaying my appointment would make some sense, but laughter? I try to make out the words, but all I can hear is mumbling. The only distinct sound is that of occasional laughter.

I get up and pour myself a glass of water. I'm not thirsty. I do this just for the sake of doing something. Then, I observe the small bubbles as they rise to the surface and fly upwards without hesitation, racing on their way to the top, towards the light, to unite with the open air in the room.

And then I hear something. Here they come. They're leaving the room. I return to the bench, a bit too quickly. Like a guilty person. What foolishness. I just got up to pour myself some water.

"Would you like some juice?" she asks, as if I were there for a dress fitting.

"No, thank you. I helped myself to some water."

Little does she care. Evidently, the fact that I've been waiting on this little bench for the last fifteen minutes didn't even deserve a hint of an apology.

"All right," she says in her calm voice, as she shows the woman who was laughing during my fifteen minutes to the door. "You may go in now."

And then, suddenly, I'm in this other room, once again waiting for her.

She shouts from the other room:

"Are you sure you wouldn't like a cup of coffee, tea, some juice, or something else?"

"No, really, I'm fine," I shout back.

In the room I see two chairs, two sofa chairs, a coffee table, more flowers, and even more of the female garbage. Flower arrangements and the like. All right, everything is quite tasteful, but it somehow makes my stomach turn.

I bet she's not coming in so she can see where I'm going to sit. But, I know that trick. I won't sit anywhere. I'll stand in the middle of the room and wait for her to come in.

And here she is, finally, with a cup of coffee in her hand.

"Where do you sit?" I ask.

"I sit here, across from you," she says and motions me to a chair.

She then spends some time observing the potted Japanese violets standing in the window, and says:

"I don't know what's wrong with them. They won't bloom like they're supposed to."

"That's odd," I say. "They certainly have enough light here."

Could it be that she too feels a little uncomfortable, or is this the standard beginning – seemingly informal? Like, we just met to talk about flowers. What would happen if I were to tell her flowers were the last thing in the world I was interested in? If I were to tell her my mother's home was always packed with rubber plants, cactuses, and by and large resembled a jungle so that we were never able to sit comfortably in any part of the apartment? What would happen if I were to say this, and if I were to ask her not to bother me with her flowers? Would that be considered impolite? What would happen if I were to tell her that I've made it a point not to have any plants in my home? And that in my opinion, plants don't find apartments pleasant at all. In fact, I think these plants are unhappy, condemned to listen to our quarrels, to watch us having bad sex, to breathe in our cigarette smoke and the scent of our bathroom fresheners, and worst of all, sometimes they're even condemned to endure light throughout the night. Plants that would have gone to sleep long ago, and dreamt about other plants. I could have told her all this, but of course, I didn't.

Finally, she sits in her chair. Her cup is in her hand. In fact, she's holding it with both hands. I've always liked it when people held their cups of coffee with both hands. It makes them seem so vulnerable. They look like someone who is trying to keep warm by holding this cup. I'm inclined to develop an instant and irrational liking to people who hold their cups in this manner.

Why is she doing this to me?

She smiles at me – a nice, warm smile. Not at all fake. Trained, maybe, but honest. It's clear she's not afraid of the silence between us. Leaning back in her sofa chair, which is, as I've just come to notice, significantly lower than mine, she slowly brings the coffee cup to her lips and takes a sip. Once again she places it in her lap, still using both hands.

"So, how are things?" she asks.

"Confusing," I say, determined to be completely honest.

Since I've already decided to pay for the aggravation, the least I could do is try to be honest.

"Confusing. Aaall right. And what else?"

"Well… to be honest, I also find it all a little silly. Unusual. I even feel a bit humiliated, but not too much."

"Why humiliated?"

"It's like, well, you should be able to solve your own problems. If you ask for help, it means you're weak. I guess?"

"Whose voice is telling you you're weak?"

The voice of my husband, I'm thinking to myself. But I don't say anything. He's the one who thinks if he can do everything on his own then everyone else should too.

"All right. Here's what I know about you. You're forty-three years old, a writer by profession, you're married… do you have any children?"

Oh, dear God. Here it comes.

"No, I don't have any children."

"Was this a mutual decision or…."

"Well, sort of, yes, I guess… we didn't really come out and say we didn't want children, but we didn't really try to have them

either. On the contrary. We made sure it didn't happen. Had I decided I wanted children, I'm sure my husband would have supported me, but since it frightens me, he, of course, never forced me to do anything that frightened me. . . ."

I shouldn't have mentioned my fear. If she now starts pestering me about this. . . .

"In any case," I quickly continued so as not to allow her to jump in with one of her questions, "I don't think this presents a major problem for me. It's quite clear now that I won't be having children and I've learned to live with it. Sometimes I feel a bit uneasy when I find myself with a group of women who have children, and they start talking about them, because I can't participate, but for the most part, it's okay."

She smiled. I got the impression that she realized I didn't wish to talk about it anymore.

I too leaned back in my sofa chair. The hell with it. I'm here. Whatever happens, happens.

"I'm afraid of this," I said.

"What exactly frightens you?"

"Pain frightens me, naturally. I know this is a process and that it will last and that it will be painful the entire time. I'm afraid of what we're going to dig up, and of all the feelings I'm

going to experience on my way there, wherever that might be. I'm afraid of giving up halfway through. I'm afraid I might even make it all the way and then reach a place not worth all the searching and all that pain. I'm afraid of all the things that might creep out in the meantime."

And then I told her all those things about the writing. How my writing used to give me great pleasure, how nothing could be more important, and how the satisfaction I felt after writing a story couldn't be compared to anything else.

"Maybe the problem is," I said, "is the fact that I've decided to write a novel. Maybe I'm expecting too much of myself, who knows. Maybe the short stories were an ideal genre for me. You lift the lid just a bit, for a few days, dig around your inner self, write the story and quickly close it again before all the demons find their way out. Open, write, close. Over and over again. And now, suddenly, a novel. This means that lid, that manhole, has to stay open for a long time. For months and months. And I have to live next to it, sit on the edge of that ravine, look down and feel my legs tremble above the abyss. To be exposed for months to the stench that is about to gush forth. And this is why I haven't written anything for the last two, three years. I tell people I'm writing a novel but, in truth, I'm doing nothing. I wander aimlessly about the apartment, clean it to no end, play computer games, write to strangers all over the world, have conversations with cyber maniacs which, had

I made notes, could have been played on Broadway that same instant, but I never bothered to write them down. That's the strangest thing of all. It's not unusual when you find it hard to do a job you never really liked. But when you suddenly can't do something you used to like, something you used to enjoy, well, then there must be a problem somewhere. This is why I came to you. Primarily because of this. I want to know why I can't write a novel."

To me this sounded like an excellent explanation. I almost believed in it myself.

Our conversation revolved around this problem a little while longer. I told her a little about my family. She posed small, pleasant questions, and I talked. About my mother, about my father, about the nice, green house where I grew up. I felt like crying again when I came to that part, but I controlled myself. She said:

"Feel free to cry."

I suddenly felt like this was all too much. I thought things would go more slowly. That it wouldn't hurt right away. I told her I have nothing against warm and open communication; that I'm willing to make an honest effort, but that I nevertheless need time to open up. I felt like I was walking on top of an enormous ball, contemplating whether or not I'm going to stay there and waste our time, or if I'm just going to dive into the depths. And I knew the latter frightened me immensely.

"I see," she said, "that you have a very pleasant way of letting others know where your boundaries are, how far they can go with you. You do this in such a way as not to hurt the other person."

I was both thrilled by her compliment as well as ashamed by the fact that such little praise could make me so happy. Could it be that I crave approval to that extent?

"Would you say your life has been a happy one so far?"

What a tough question! Is there anyone who can honestly say they are happy? And as far as the other question goes, the one about the meaning of happiness, I don't even want to think about it, let alone discuss it. It's so overdone.

"Hmm… I don't really know. Let's just say that the only thing I can tell you for certain is that, so far, my life has not been an unhappy one. I've been blessed with so many things. Compared to other people, I've fared well. I'm not ill. I'm not an invalid. I'm not unattractive. I have the right number of fingers and toes. I didn't have to experience the things I truly dread, like being born in a town consisting of ten houses stacked on top of each other on some mountain somewhere. For me, that is the worst imaginable fate, even though this might not be the case.

But, when I travel somewhere and see such places and houses, and think about the people who live there, I know I'm very lucky I'm not one of them. Compared to the people who are really unhappy, I guess I'm happy. I don't know."

A small clock stood in the window, sideways, strategically positioned so that I could see it, and be aware of how my time was running out much faster than I would like it to. I remember the operation from two years ago. That was easy. You go in, they put you out, remove a few gallstones, which caused you unbearable pain, and – you come out healthy. Sheer magic. How great would it be if the therapist could do the same.

"And if therapy did work like this," she asked, "what would you like to change?"

Finally, an easy question.

I blurted out, all in one breath, a few hundred of my faults. Then I stopped myself halfway through because it was clear that the surgical removal of just the first half would mean a great deal.

"You know," she smiled, "those who love themselves are inclined to forgive themselves for their faults. I wouldn't want you to have unrealistic expectations regarding therapy. Therapy may

not be able to help you fix everything you might consider a fault, but it can help you to accept it. To be at peace with it. To discover things about yourself that are unique and then embrace them, love them, and live with them."

I wanted to jump up and kiss her.

However, my time was up, and while I was getting ready to get up and leave, she began telling me about how we were going to start with about ten sessions and then see how we were getting on, and whether or not all this had any sense.

"Actually," I said at the door, "that would be really devastating, to hear you tell me after a few sessions that you no longer wish to be my therapist because I'm a lost cause."

She laughed, honestly, as she was showing me out.

You idiot, why do you feel the need to make your therapist laugh?

As I was driving home, my cheeks were burning and I had a minor headache, but I kept thinking about how absolutely wonderful her last comment was. She is someone who gives me permission to be who I am. No better, no worse. I don't think I've had anything like that with anyone in my entire life. Even if she wasn't one-hundred-percent honest, even if there was a hidden motive behind her permission, it was still nice of her to say it. It was as though she told me I was just fine, no matter what I was like. The point was to find out what I was really like. This, perhaps, didn't have to be that difficult?

THREE

A situation like this one:

It's almost midnight. I get into bed wishing to forget everything about the day as quickly as possible. Tomorrow everything will reappear, there's no doubt about that. Still, I'll be safe for a few hours. Sleep is awesome. Insomnia is one of the rare things I've never had trouble with. I sink into a deep sleep as though it were a pleasant thought. As though I were going under anaesthesia. I just choose to sleep and, there I am, on the other side, already gone.

The remote is in place. I usually flick through the channels a little before falling asleep. Might as well be honest, I know only too well that porn movies start a quarter after midnight on cable. I don't know how you feel about them, but they always do a good job of putting me to sleep. Ten minutes of porn; oh that's plenty! More than enough. They can go on to develop their plot for as long as they like – I'll be fast asleep. And so, while flicking through the channels, because the porn movie won't start for another five minutes, I come across my old love. There he is, walking around in a hat and long coat, the same Bogart wannabe from fifteen years ago, the one I was so crazy about and the reason I imagined I was the victim of Jupiter gone mad, Hank Chinaski's mistress, Ingrid Bergman herself, while also being ugly, like the famous hunchback of the even more famous church in Paris, the reincarnation of Ernest Hemingway, born only to amuse and mesmerize him, just like Aska enchanted her wolf, which I did well for a while. But only for a while. Wolves are there to eat you, no doubt about that. They're not there to bake cookies with you for the rest of your life, or hold the yarn for you while you wind it into a ball.

Well, that's the guy walking across the TV screen and talking about how this city has been destroyed by vulgarity, the invasion of primitive people, and the lack of taste of nobodies who were born to this world due to a mistake of nature. And he's saying all this right when I want to watch my ten minutes of porn, do what's supposed be done during this time, and then calmly and peacefully fall asleep.

It's not too pleasant when you realize, with your hand down your pajamas, that you had spent half your youth loving a trained fascist, disguised as a man of renaissance beauty.

What do I watch now?

A little of both?

Channel one: He's reciting some sort of self-loving monologue in front of a mirror in the last remaining watering hole in the old part of the city, whining over the bulldozers that are going to tear everything down first thing tomorrow, after which someone else will come to cover the demolished shrine with modern and estranged chrome.

Channel fifteen: They don't have a problem with bad taste here. They're all wearing tiger and leopard print lingerie, together with 12-inch heels, the most horrible wigs ever, silicone breasts, and they're ready for action.

Channel one: He's walking along a river and grieving for the fish that are slowly losing their habitat because, alas, all of the remaining embankments have been occupied by boat restaurant owners. I have no intention of thinking about this now, the subject is boring and not at all erotic, but, damn it, we spent so many hours on these boats, arguing and making up. I recognize the hand motion. Even though he has aged. Both he and his hand. And my hand, probably. He once told me that I had child-like hands, that he noticed this while we were making love; that he looked up at my hands and thought: My God, I'm making love to a child. And now look, that child and that hand are cheating on you with third-rate porn, click, go away....

Channel fifteen: Not fair. Whenever I switch to them, she's giving him a blowjob. Why is all porn made only for men?

Channel one: He's wearing his wise-disgusted-embittered expression. An expression of a man who knows something others can't see yet. An expression of a man who has already endured Weltschmertz in place of all those living in ignorance. An expression of a man who was aware of the beauty of unformed stone before Michelangelo and who had grasped the horror, which was to follow, before the mayor of Hiroshima. The million dollar question is: Why does this expression still mean something to me even though I've been aware of its fraudulence for more than a decade? Is there a way we can ever truly get over an old love?

Channel fifteen: That's better. They're lying on a bed and kissing. I try to ignore the fact that she's still wearing the heels. And that she has long, purple nails. Because, if I focus on the details, there goes the fun.

And then, like in a bad SF movie, the painting on the wall above their bed takes me straight back to....

Channel one: Do you remember? Of course you do. You can use that expression of disgust to show off till your dying day. But such things are never forgotten. Who cares about the fate of a tennis court built in the wrong place. I'm asking you, do you remember the hotel room with the same cheap painting on the wall. Aha?! I got you now, Romeo.

Fifteen: He has grabbed her from behind and is holding her breasts firmly while thrusting himself into her, and thrusting and thrusting. Now their phone is going to ring, I'm sure of it.

One: And then the phone rang, remember, and you wouldn't stop, you just answered it and spoke to the woman from the travel agency while I thought I was going to have to bite into the pillow if you didn't hurry up and end the conversation.

Fifteen: Their phone didn't ring.

One: …threw the phone on the floor….

Fifteen: He is turning her around and looking at her and spreading her legs.

One: …he is turning me around and looking at me and spreading my legs….

A little bell in my head is screaming that he never even loved me the right way.

But too late.

Too late.

I fell asleep.

Get lost. All of you. Leopard prints. Clever. Culturally enlightened. Filled with silicone. His silicone vanity. Sticking out abnormally above all the other heads that naturally tilt downwards. His built-up ego wrapped in a perfectly pressed shirt. And why do they always smear the sperm all over their faces and breasts in the end? Are they marking their territory? What is it, damn it? I'll never be able to understand.

Click.

Go away.

FOUR

There is an old photograph of my mother and me: We're sleeping, both with curlers in our hair. She's wearing a thin, summer nightgown, which is rolled up around her thighs considerably, and I'm only in my bathing suit bottom. We're lying on a king sized bed in some rented room at the seaside. I'm, let's say, five or six-years-old. This means my mother is barely thirty. At that moment, my father is also thirty and he is watching us taking an afternoon nap in a house on the seaside, tired from swimming all morning and being out in the sun.

I try to picture him: A thirty-year-old man watching his wife and daughter. A scene both tender and erotic. And comical, of course, because of our curlers. He's probably bored. He reads the newspaper and then takes out his little magnetic chess set and plays out the game published that day. Now he's sitting there, waiting for us to wake up so that he can take us out for ice cream. What made him want to take a picture of us? What were his feelings at the time? Did he wake us up as soon as he took the picture? Were we awakened by the sound of the camera? Did my mother look at my father sleepily and say something like:

"Are you crazy? Taking a picture of me half-naked?"

But still, more than anything I would like to know: What was he feeling while he was taking our picture? For, if he took the picture because of something other than mere boredom, then I'm inclined to think that maybe we could have found a way to be happy after all. And we weren't. I hope you're not going to say he took our picture only so that he could make fun of my mother later? Or so that he could, from that moment on, claim that the two of us were only different versions of one and the same principle?

If this were a movie, whose main concern was for the characters to ultimately find peace, I would go to my father, reconcile with him, after so many years, and ask him about the photograph. And he would remember everything. He would say something like:

"Yes, I remember. Dubrovnik, 1966. The blinds were half drawn and the two of you looked so beautiful and peaceful in your sleep. I wanted to eternalize that moment of beauty because I knew it could never be repeated in the exact same way again. You were there, the two people I loved more than anything in the world...."

We'll stop here. Both you and I know things like this don't happen in real life. Not in your life, right? Nor in mine, believe me.

In real life, I will never find out even the basic facts like: Where we were vacationing; what year it was exactly; whether or not the break-up was already a subject of conversation, or if it just hovered over our plastic plates on the beach.

In real life, I certainly wouldn't go to my father. And if I did, a conversation about an old photograph would not be possible.

In real life, we would only get into another argument, over something trivial and with a certain outcome.

I remember there was a dirt road near that house, leading down to the beach, and that all the shrubbery was dry and scorched by the sun. I remember the small branches of these bushes were completely covered in miniature snails, which were hanging on the twigs like buds. I remember taking one of those branches back with me to the room and how, by the next morning, the little snails crawled all over our beds, chairs, the floor, our clothing. And I remember my parents being extremely angry with me because of this. That photograph and those snails, I could almost swear it all happened precisely then, that summer. They were angry the entire time. And it was always my fault. And from then on, whenever I go to the seaside and I see small snails stuck to dry twigs, the same feeling of sadness comes flooding back.

And since you insist, I also remember this:

Last summer I was tidying up my garden. It was one of those ordinary summer days. A Sunday, probably, because only on a Sunday can I be compelled to take a broom into my hands and clear the fallen leaves for lack of a better idea.

I wandered a little deeper into the grass. I took one wrong step. And then I heard: crack!

A broken snail shell was right under my foot. Half of the shell was smashed. The snail, which was most likely injured, was curled up in the remaining half. What would you do with a broken snail? How would you feel? Do you think this is a good enough reason to shed so many tears? And did I really solve anything by picking it up and throwing it far into the neighbouring backyard? All right, it's not going to die at my door, but does that really change anything?

This was one of those arguments my husband could not explain. He reconciled himself to the fact that this was probably one of those days of the month when women go mad.

I burst in there with a fury, straight from an argument with my mother. The lady whose session, as I've now come to realize, regularly runs into mine, is in there and once again I have my fifteen minutes on the little bench. But that's all right, I'll be taking fifteen minutes from the person who comes in after me and we'll be even. We all get our share, only with a slight delay. This reminds me of something, but I can't deal with that now, I'm too angry.

I know exactly what will happen. If I tell her I got into an argument with my mother just before coming here, she'll think this definitely wasn't a coincidence. Allowing my mother to get me so upset before leaving for my session? Maybe it isn't a coincidence? I could have simply cut short our phone conversation and stopped insisting to that nonsense. But no! I couldn't make myself stop until the whole thing turned into me screaming into the phone and her whining on the subject of why I'm so rude to her and why I'm torturing her. Damn it! Damn it! Damn it! I'm sitting here and gasping for breath and waiting for them to let me in so that I can start complaining about my mother. Outside, it's the most beautiful spring day imaginable; I could be doing so many other things instead of sitting in the waiting room of a therapist, anxious to start beating on the one who gave me life. I remember the dark spots that are starting to show on my mother's face. They've become larger over the years, and I always look closely to see if they're getting bigger too quickly or as quickly as they should. I remember how concerned I am about her well being.

Unless my concern is also a mask for something else, something I don't even dare say out loud.

Here they are, they're coming out, and now I already know where to sit. This time, I won't be examining the Japanese violets. While still at the door, she asks me how I am and I start talking before I even sit down. I tell her this visit is like going to an emergency room. She looks at me, uncertain as to whether she should smile at this remark or not. I smile, to let her know it was a joke. An exaggeration. All right, you can smile, it won't hurt my feelings. I say:

"Shortly before coming here, I got into a terrible argument with my mother."

She looked at me curiously.

"It's obvious, of course, that we're going to have to talk about it, because now my mood is tainted by this, and I doubt I could talk about anything else."

I'm grateful to her for not asking what the argument was

about. One single argument isn't important. They're all important, I guess. I say:

"She always manages to push me into the same state: I start screaming at her like a child, and I don't know whether I'm more angry with her for doing this to me, or with myself for always reacting in the same way. Why can't I tell her what I think in a nice, calm, adult manner and leave it at that? Why?"

She gets up and takes a sketching pad and some magic markers from the table. She places them in my lap and says:

"Imagine this situation with your mother was a comic strip. What sort of comic strip would it be? Draw it!"

"But I don't know how to draw!"

"It doesn't matter, draw it any way you can."

"I draw like a three-year-old."

"That's not important. Draw the first thing that comes to your mind."

And here I am, drawing: A big elephant and a small elephant, and a bucket of water between the two.

At first she thinks the small elephant is me, but I explain to her it's the other way around. I'm the big elephant. The small elephant is my mother. The small elephant is standing behind the big elephant.

"What are the two elephants doing?" she asks.

"The big elephant performs in a circus. It's very busy, the audience is waiting for it, the circus is packed and it needs to get ready for its big act. The small elephant is getting in its way, it's pushing this bucket filled with water under its feet, it wants to give it some water, it's going to trip it…."

"What does the small elephant say to the big one?"

"It says: Take the water from the bucket, it's good for you, it's the only thing that's good for you, all the other things people will try to give you are no good, I know some of the people from the audience will offer you candy and peanuts, but you shouldn't take it because it's not clean. Only the things I give you are good for you."

"What does the big elephant say to this?"

"The big elephant says: Leave me alone, you pesky little elephant! I have a serious job ahead of me, I have to work; the whole circus is waiting for me, while you're pestering me with that bucket, which is, by the way, bigger than you. You can't even move it and still you won't let it be! There's no way you're going to make me drink the water, you're just getting in my way."

"If this comic strip had a name, what would it be?"

"A Useless Attempt!" I replied, right off the bat.

I had no idea where this was coming from. Any of it. Those elephants, that bucket, or the "useless attempt." It just burst out of me all at once. And the worst part of all was that I didn't feel any shame whatsoever.

"Whose attempt was useless?"

"Well, the small elephant's attempt to make the big elephant drink from the bucket was useless."

"All right, what does the small elephant say next?"

"It says: If it wasn't for me, you would never have become such a big elephant, you wouldn't be performing in a circus, you would never have come this far, never stood under a spotlight as people applaud you… and now you're pushing me away."

"The big elephant?"

"The big elephant says: Leave me alone, go over there with the other small elephants."

"And the small one?"

"The small one says there are no other small elephants. It's the only one there."

"So, the small elephant is alone?"

"Yes, all alone."

"What does the big elephant say to that?"

"It doesn't say anything. It also realizes there are no other small elephants."

"How does the big elephant feel now?"

"It's sad. Very sad."

"What would happen if the big elephant also went on its way and left the small elephant?"

"A catastrophe. The small elephant would kill itself. It would drown itself in the bucket of water. For sure."

"So, there's no solution?"

"No."

"Then whose attempt is useless?"

I know, I know, all right. I got it. You don't have to keep jabbing the screwdriver into my kidneys.

I remember how, at the beginning of this session, I told her I didn't want to repeat the concept of women-martyrs, which runs in our family so naturally, as though it belonged there and nowhere else. Now I get the urge to bash my head against the wall and swallow my own words, along with everything else I said about the years I spent analysing my mother's behavior. Questions like: why she does the things she does, how her parents treated her, whether or not she got the love she needed, how she felt when she got a younger brother, and whether or not she was forced to grow up too soon. I heard her say many times that she never had time to be a child. My mother doesn't like cartoons. She doesn't have a great sense of humor. And she loves talking about illnesses and potential catastrophes. This is all because the child within her is acting like a grown-up, I explained to my therapist.

"It's odd," she said, "how much effort you put into finding excuses for her...."

"You don't understand! By searching for excuses for her, I was actually searching for something that would make me feel better. Because, if she's behaving the way she is because something was also missing from her childhood, then her behavior is not directed towards me. Then it's just the result of her own personal pain, then she didn't really have a choice!"

I was practically screaming.

"All right, I understand that, but it's still a bit odd. When did you switch roles? Usually it's the parents who look for excuses to justify the actions of their children. Only in rare cases do the children think about their parents in this way."

What is she trying to say? That my mother is behaving as though she was my spoiled, selfish, capricious child whose actions I'm trying to justify? I was persistent.

"She is the one who benefits from this. It's her game. She always has to be in the right. If she upsets me, she benefits. If I don't let on that she had upset me, she benefits again because she knows it's an act and that I'm just suppressing my anger. She wins either way."

"And what do you get out of it?"

"Me!?"

"Yes. What do you get out of it? If this is a recurring pattern of behavior, then you too must also be getting something out of it."

I stared at her, not knowing what to say. What the fuck do I get out of it? High blood pressure? An ulcer? Chewed up nails? A big phone bill? What?

"I don't know," I said. "I really don't know. I never really thought I got anything out of it. Do you have any suggestions?"

"The truth is only what you perceive to be the truth."

"Yes, but still… you probably have some idea…."

"I can only assume, but it doesn't necessarily mean I'm right."

"All right. Tell me what you think."

Sometimes, we ask a question knowing we'll get an answer we don't want to hear. And still, we ask. We can't help ourselves.

She looked me straight in the eyes and said:

"Pain. That's what you get out of it. Pain. You're used to it and that's why you repeat the pattern over and over again. To get your portion of pain and uphold the family tradition of the woman-martyr."

I was silent, I don't know for how long. Maybe a minute or two. Maybe much longer. To me, it seemed like I was quiet for a long time, and she didn't interfere. I stared at the small and the big elephant without saying anything. Finally, I looked up and asked:

"All right, how do I stop doing this? How do I get better?"

She placed her cup on the table, sighed, and said:

"By doing just this. By talking about it."

FIVE

"It is possible to resist the effects of pheromones, unless you're under the influence of alcohol," says a clever girl on TV.

I guess she just assumes we want to resist the pheromones.

There were a few more excellent sentences. Something about how it's a good thing we're not in love all the time because, if this were the case, many of us would die of sexual exhaustion, followed by the futility of bathing. In other words, you can wash away all scents, but not the cunning pheromones! For your information, there is a small organ at the top of the nose, which can detect them regardless of the amount of expensive perfume you use.

And wait till you hear this statement: "Romantic love begins taking root in our brains even as far back as our earliest childhood!?" According to the girl on television, this is called a neurological correlate, whatever that is, and it basically means that we form a picture of the one we will later fall in love with very early in our childhood.

So, I can stop blaming myself, and my neurotic and inconsistent taste in men. My childhood is to blame, as always. First, some sort of picture was formed in my childhood (I'm not responsible, that's general knowledge, go to my parents if you don't like the picture) and then, while walking calmly along without suspecting a thing, I ran into someone's pheromones and – click. I basically have very little to do with this, right? And, if on top of that, I was under the influence of alcohol, which is quite possible, then I also have scientific evidence proving that I couldn't resist myself – several times, in fact.

Pheromones. Under the influence of pheromones, I once wallpapered an entire room and painted the kitchen chairs red, all by myself! Today, I can't even get myself to do the dusting or iron his shirts. I also used to put a few drops of perfume along with the detergent when I did the wash – my little trick; a way for him to always feel like I'm by his side.

We painted the apartment together and sat on the floor, all dirty, drank beer, and then made love on some old newspaper because the furniture was pushed together in the middle of the room and covered with sheets. Today, there's so much to watch on television, work to be done for tomorrow, and then there's the fatigue, that, in fact, isn't really fatigue but more a state of mind. All in all, I'd rather go to sleep, my darling. You turn the lights off and just quietly crawl into bed later, after all your work is done....

It's not always like that, of course. Don't write me off so easily. Still, I don't know how you deal with these thoughts. I myself have a hard time with them. In my head there's always a saboteur on call who, at a certain moment, pushes me into thinking about diseases.

For example, my husband and I are making love.

He runs his hand over my breasts.

I'm thinking about that commercial: Visit your oncologist every six months, blah, blah, blah.... I haven't seen my oncologist in ten years. Who knows what could be growing inside me. There, I can feel it here, under my fingers. Even under his fingers. But, truth be told, I can always feel something. After you pass the age of forty, you start getting lumpier anyway, and then you don't know which lumps should be there and which shouldn't.

And this is how it is with every part of your body.

I can hear my lungs wheezing. Cigarettes.

I feel a pain in my right hip as I raise my legs.

And I wonder what it's going to be like in the next ten or twenty years.

Sex reminds me more and more of general body deterioration. More explicitly, of death. Hospital smells. The callous faces of the doctors. The instruments they shove into your body shouting: "Relax, for God's sake, I can't examine you!" Meanwhile, I could never relax in their examination rooms, and even here, I find it increasingly difficult to do so.

Where can you get pheromones at four in the morning? Can they buy pheromones at the corner drugstore, let's say, in the States? Is there someone willing to inject you with them at this hour, to end your withdrawals? Why don't they sell bottled cocktails containing pheromones, serotonins, dopamine, and other hormones that make us happy? Is it all really that trivial, simply chemicals playing around with my brain which then sends signals to the body telling it to lie listlessly, or jump around, or sleep, or shrivel from weakness? Do I get a say in all this?

This is not exactly how I pictured myself growing old. I thought middle age would be different. That it would eliminate fear. Eliminate the wavering. That absolute control would take the place of indecision. I thought the order of things would somehow be established naturally and painlessly, telling us precisely how to deal with each part of our body and our every thought.

But, I haven't experienced anything of the kind. The only difference is that now everyone expects more from you. And no one is prepared to make any allowances for anything you do because you are young.

Maybe this is why I'm trying to run directly from youth into old age in such a panic. I'm in urgent need of new extenuating circumstances. Something new I can use to justify myself. I'm sorry, but I'm not ready for this new you-are-held-accountable-for-your-actions situation. And I don't think I ever will be. Besides, why should I even be held responsible for my actions if everything is – we heard it loud and clear – just a game played out by our hormones and the pictures created in our childhood? Maybe, if we're clever enough, we'll be able to combine these pictures in a more useful way. Is that it? That's a laugh! I'd like to see you do it! And we'll line up the hormones in rows and then use them according to need, circumstances, and as the situation dictates. Right.

I give up.

I trust that in my lifetime, a few people will love me enough not to leave me, in spite of everything.

I trust that all of the fears haunting us don't necessarily have to come true. Or is that precisely what's going to happen?

I trust that I will die before I even realize I'm dying.

I trust that tomorrow will be a nice, sunny day and that I'll forget all this.

Above all, I trust in the pheromones. There must be another large supply somewhere. All we have to do is locate it in our brains, dig them up, and let them jump around as they did before.

I trust in the ability of self-deception.

I trust in the new diet, and the face and breast lift cream.

I trust that, because today I felt no aches and pains, it's probably all in my head, as usual.

I trust that the movie I'm going to watch tonight will be interesting enough to distract me from my thoughts for two hours. And that no one waiting in line behind me will start to cough and remind me again of death. And that there won't be a lonely, old lady sitting in the back row to make me feel deep and helpless sorrow.

I trust in the fact that this is not the first time I feel this way.

"I want to tell you about the dream I had last night. I think it might be important."

She nodded.

"In this dream, my mother is giving birth. I'm there somewhere, nearby, watching. I'm even giving my mother some useful tips. I tell her to lie on her side because that'll make it easier for her to squeeze the baby out. I think about how everything is going smoothly and without any problems, how very brave my mother is, and how she's not making a sound. At one moment, the baby starts coming out of my mother's body. It's inside of a kind of semi-transparent membrane, similar to a balloon, but I can see its face and I'm very excited. The baby's head is coming out – the baby opens its eyes and looks directly at me! Then, the doctors take the baby out and place it on the table next to my mother. The baby is still inside the membrane and I'm worried about whether it's going to start crying, whether it's even alive. It seems like no one intends to remove the membrane from the baby. Finally, we hear a faint cry, but it sounds like it's coming from a distance, because the baby still hasn't inhaled the outside air, only the air inside

its membrane. I'm worried, and I ask someone if the baby is going to be all right. Someone answers me: Yes, the baby will be fine, but I can't say the same for the mother. At that moment, I look at my mother again, and I see them putting towels between her legs to collect the gushing blood. This is where the dream ends."

"All right," she says, "which part of the dream was most significant to you?"

"The moment when the baby looked at me. And then, my concern about whether the baby was going to be all right, whether it was going to live."

"And the least significant?"

"Well, probably the fact that it was my mother who was giving birth. In my dream, this was normal to me, not at all unusual."

"Now try to imagine that you are the baby being born. You're inside the membrane, you open your eyes, and… what do you see?"

"I see a face smiling at me, the face of someone close to me. I see someone who is concerned about me."

"Good. Now they put you down on a table. You're still inside the membrane. What are you thinking now?"

"I'm thinking about how I can't wait for them to remove the membrane. I want to be able to move around more. I want to breathe in the fresh air. I want to hear every sound, and experience the richness of every color and scent. This membrane is restricting me."

"All right," she says again as she makes one of her usual gestures – when she slides her hand from her forehead to her nose, moving slowly down to her lips. "Now go back inside yourself, the self that is watching the baby on the table. What would you say to that baby?"

"I would say: You're small and weak and you need to be extra careful until you grow up. All options are open to you, you haven't made any mistakes yet, and you're like a brand new notebook that has yet to be filled. I'll help you avoid making the same mistakes I made."

"And what does the baby say to that?"

"The baby is strangely wise. Even though she has had no previous life experiences, she seems to possess some sort of innate knowledge. The baby says: Everyone needs to make their own mistakes. You can't protect me from that."

"Aha," she says with a little smile, which I don't know how to interpret. "So this is a wise baby."

"Yes," I say, at the risk of being mocked by her. "It's a wise baby."

"Then what do you say to the wise baby?"

"I tell her that that's not completely true. That not everyone has to go through the entire repertoire of mistakes. Some can be left out. All we need to do is find the right way to explain how to avoid them to someone still young. I would tell the baby I didn't have anyone to tell me this, but that now she has me."

"Aha. So, you're not giving up and you're prepared to teach the baby. Do you like teaching in general?"

"No, no I don't," I try to defend myself. "I've never taught anyone in my life."

I know this is a lie. But at this moment, I don't want to be someone who teaches.

"You mentioned some mistakes. Which mistakes were you referring to? What are the things you don't want the baby to repeat?"

I think about this for a while. I try to come up with something original, something worthy of a writer, but my mind won't budge an inch from the banal. All right, I think to myself, if the essence of life lies in banality and stereotypes, then let's say it all out loud.

"I wouldn't want this baby to suffer because of people who are not worthy of it. I want it to love itself, to be good to itself first, and then others. To be happy."

She gets up, takes a pillow from one of the chairs, and throws it on the floor in front of me. Then she says:

"Imagine that this is the baby. It's lying there in its membrane. Now, try to imagine that you are the membrane. What is its role, what do you think the membrane would say?"

"But the membrane is not alive," I say. "It's made of some kind of matter that's similar to parchment, it's taut and brittle. If someone were to pierce it, just once, it would crumble and disappear."

"Nevertheless," she insists, "if that parchment-like membrane could say something, what would it be? Anything, just say the first thing that comes to your mind...."

I've never done anything so silly in my life, there's no doubt about it. I'm a parchment-like membrane, which is preventing a baby from taking a breath of fresh air. What do I want to say? What?

"I'm the membrane and I have power. My power is short-

lived, but while it lasts, it's enormous."

She asks me again:

"What is the basis of your power?"

"This baby is mine and mine only. No one else can see it clearly."

"Perhaps there's also something good in this membrane, something useful?"

"Yes, I protect this baby from the outside world. I provide a kind of transitional period between the time spent in the mother's womb, and complete exposure to the world."

She's on her feet now, walking around the room. She throws a glance at me and then at the pillow-baby on the floor – like someone who is trying to come up with a plan. She thinks she's close to discovering something, but I already know that she won't succeed. I don't know how, I just know.

"Look at this baby. Go back inside yourself and look at it. Try to picture its future, its character, its destiny. What will it be like, what kind of person will it turn out to be?"

Until a moment ago, I was protecting it, because it's fragile and tiny and pure. But suddenly, I know; I know exactly what it'll be like, and I know it doesn't really need my protection. I say:

"In time, the baby will become a rather haughty girl, pretty, self-confident, narcissistic; she'll be tall and she'll have long, black hair. In fact, I'm afraid she's even going to be a little shallow. She won't be described as being overly sophisticated. People will like her and she will consider this to be completely normal. She will think she is entitled to all these things."

She is still looking down at the pillow and then, in a voice that clearly indicates that, for her, this is a major moment in our session today, she says:

"Can you still set her free? Can you make the decision to pierce the membrane even though the baby will become all those things: shallow, haughty, narcissistic…? Will you let her live or will you leave her to die in this parchment-like bubble?"

All of a sudden, all this seems silly to me. I start thinking about how things aren't quite as simple as she would like them to be. I hesitate and she's aware of that. Finally, I say:

"From a rational point of view, there's no way in the world I'd leave any baby to die, if I had any say in it. But, if you regard this baby as a part of me, the part I'm not setting free, and I believe this is your theory, right? Then I'm afraid things aren't quite that simple. If it were that simple, people wouldn't be spending years going to therapy. Besides, I strongly feel that it's not my job at all to free this baby from its membrane. Someone

else is supposed to do it, and don't ask me who because I don't know. All I know is that it can't be me! And I know it's not that simple!"

"I think it is all up to you," she said, going back to sit in her chair. "It's your decision and yours only."

I didn't say anything. I felt like I might have gone a bit too far. As if I had said something against her therapeutic magic. As if I had displayed unseemly doubt. But, damn it, I can't feign a breakthrough just to make her feel better! It would be asking too much, right?

I looked at the clock. I had another ten minutes left. A whole eternity! She seemed tired all of a sudden, sitting there in her sofa chair. It was late and I was probably her last patient for the day. I said:

"I believe you're tired."

Even if she were, she would never admit to it. And she didn't. She said:

"No, I'm not at all tired, I'm completely focused and you have my full attention."

"I don't think so. I think you'd rather be someplace else, perhaps with your children. Do you have any children?"

She nodded quickly, too quickly, as if to say that who she is outside this room should under no circumstances be the subject of our conversation.

"Where did that come from, that concern for the way I feel? The other day you asked me if I wanted to take a break between sessions. Why are you being so considerate?"

"I don't know. I think you find me tiresome. You're probably listening to me only because it's your job, because I'm paying you to listen, while you'd much rather be someplace else and with other people."

I was on the verge of tears. I knew exactly what was happening to me, but I wasn't able to stop it. What did I really want from her? To tell me that she was listening to me because she liked me and not because she was being paid? There was no end to the self-pity. It was obvious I was going to use every last minute of my session. I leaned a little towards her. I think she likes it when I pose a question as if I believe she possesses all the wisdom of the world. Hell, who doesn't?

"What do you think, do I really need therapy? Could it be that I'm just indulging a whim, some sort of eccentricity, snobbery, the same as if I had, let's say, enrolled myself in a horseback riding school...."

"Something that narcissistic baby would do?" she asked with a smile.

"Seriously, do you think I need this?"

I knew the answer in advance. She, of course, thinks all people need therapy, that it's something that would benefit everyone.

"…but, if you're asking me whether you're a serious case…."

I interrupted her in the middle of this sentence. And I should have let her continue. I'll never find out if I'm a serious case. Or at least not until next week, which is when I'll see her again.

"No, that's not what I was asking you. I was referring to whether or not I was entitled to this. And why I feel guilty now for taking up your time, and why I feel guilty for doing something I enjoy."

"This baby," she looked at the pillow on the floor again, "she wouldn't feel guilty for receiving something?"

"Not a bit. This baby has no problems with taking."

It was time for me to get up and leave. I knew that and so did she.

As we take out our notepads to write down the date and time of our next session, I tell her that now I make notes of everything that happens during our talks.

"You may find yourself in a novel."

But, we are no longer in that room and she is no longer my therapist. Or at least that's what I think. She is showing me out and at the door she says:

"I hope I'm going to be a positive figure."

"Don't worry," I say, "all the characters are positive, except me. That's something that never changes."

SIX

Dare you to guess: Who, out of all the people riding in this streetcar this morning, is going to die of lung cancer?

I know two will die. It's not for certain when, but two definitely. That's what the statistics say.

Three will die of a heart attack. At least.

This is an interesting game you can play while using public transportation. Study their faces, fingers. Are their fingers yellow from nicotine, or are their noses abnormally red, or are they gasping for air as they climb into the bus, or do they have that empty suicidal stare?

I sometimes close my eyes when I drive my car and count.

My record is nine. And I do this at night, crossing a bridge, when I know the road is empty and straight. Which really isn't much of an achievement.

Did you know that people sometimes wake up in the middle of an operation? The most terrifying part of all is that you have no way of letting anyone know you're awake. They're cutting you and digging around your insides and you can feel everything, but you can't let out a scream. This has happened to people, only no one talks about it. This is the dark secret of operating rooms.

Let's say you're lying on a beach somewhere. Everything around you is idyllic. You even look rather good in your bathing suit. And you also managed to find some shade. You're reading a newspaper while resting comfortably on your beach mattress. You feel like nothing bad could happen to you here. And then, a tiny, little, black ant just happens to walk into your ear. It wanders around and you try to get it out with you finger, but you're only pushing it farther and deeper into your head. The ant is moving straight to your brain. This has happened to people. After a while, you think you imagined it all and that there was no ant after all. You continue to calmly read your newspaper and lie in the sun. But, the ant begins to make a nest in your head, to lay eggs, and multiply. By the time you eat two ice-cream cones, there will be an ant colony inside your head, which is going to kill you slowly and painfully. There's no cure. Now try enjoying yourself on the beach. Or anywhere for that matter.

I know a man who cut his eye on a newspaper, while he was reading the latest news and resting comfortably on his couch one afternoon.

I leave my house in the morning and I think: if the first car I run into is white, that means I'll die within five years at the most. If the car isn't white but some other color, then I get another chance, which, however, also comes with a catch. I have to add all the numbers on the license plate and if the sum is an odd number, then I'm saved. At least for the day. At least for the morning.

If a new move opens up in a game of solitaire, I won't get a brain tumor.

If it doesn't, then I'll tell myself this is just a sick game I play on my own to make myself feel bad. Why would anyone intentionally do something that makes him or her (or them) feel bad, is that what you're asking? What an absurd question. And you, I suppose, don't do such things? Haven't you ever imagined your own miserable end in some old-age home? When I really think about it, an old age home is the deluxe version. It would be more correct to say: your own miserable end in some dreadfully dirty apartment, which hasn't been aired for months and which no one comes to visit anymore. Don't tell me you've never read an article like: Elderly man found dead in his apartment. Estimated time of death: approximately six months prior to discovery. Neighbors have been complaining about an unpleasant odor in the hallway for some time. And you never think this could one day be you? I always do.

SEVEN

I don't know exactly when I made the decision not to have children. Or if it even was a decision or just one of those things you keep putting off indefinitely, knowing full well the time that you have is limited. Maybe only fifteen, twenty years at the most. And then, you suddenly realize that the decision is no longer up to you. You definitely can't have them, even if you wanted to. Stories like: A woman in India gave birth at the age of sixty! Both mother and infant are healthy and doing fine.... You somehow know this doesn't apply to you and that this is just a newspaper article.

Was this another one of those decisions I tend to make for the sole purpose of making myself feel bad?

Either way, that's how it turned out.

It's not that bad for now. We have our time. And time is one of the rare things a person can actually have. We have our afternoons and our weekends. We have order in our kitchen and neatly stacked shelves. We never had to use the washing machine twice a day because of dirty diapers. Nor did we have to get out of bed ten times during the night. You don't think that's really a plus? Okay. Maybe you're right. I'm just presenting my arguments.

Your family and friends resign themselves to the idea when you reach your late thirties. This is when they definitely lose all hope.

But, there are always those times when you need to get your hair done.

In hair salons, most of the talk is about children. Photographs are taken out. Pregnant women get their hair done out of turn. There's mention of C-sections, pelvic births, measles, baby-teeth are shown around, and sometimes even the children are brought in to get their hair cut with their mothers, at which time we all have to sigh and cry oh, he's so cute and swear the child is the spitting image of its mother.

I've yet to see a woman who comes into a salon and talks

about her ill mannered, full-grown child. I've never heard a woman talk about how her son had to repeat a grade, as she was getting a perm. Or how he robbed a corner store. Or how he started taking drugs. Or how he beat up a neighbor. Or how he can't get into college. Or how he moved to another continent and calls only once a year, just to ask for money.

In a hair salon, children exist solely in their angelic form. A form that only gives rise to plain, unadulterated envy. A form which makes you want to get out of there, with the curlers still in your hair, but not before you apologize to everyone for being there, even though you're not worthy of their company. Because they, these women, know something that you don't. And they have felt something you never will.

They are a family. You are a couple, at the most.

A girl, roughly seventeen years old, is combing my hair. She's looking at me in the mirror; I'm looking at her in the mirror. The women around us are showing photographs. I'm silent. I'm always silent in these situations, hoping no one will ask me anything. Hoping I'll be able to misrepresent myself for an hour to an hour and a half, until my hair is done, and then run out of there. But no! At some point, the girl can no longer stand the silence and she starts up a conversation with a question that, to her, seemed the least unpleasant. She also undoubtedly saw the wedding band on my finger.

"Are you married?" she asks.

What I would really like to say is be quiet and keep combing because I know what will follow, but I've never said that before, and I probably never will. Do you also sometimes find yourself in a situation when you have a thousand prepared answers, but you never say them out loud because you're deterred by sheer cowardice? Of course, you're deluding yourself with the idea that your good manners are preventing you from doing this, but, if you really think about it, you'll realize this has nothing to do with manners. It's simply cowardice. Fear of confrontation. And so you agree to their unmasking game instead of protecting your territory.

"Yes," I say with a casual smile.

And before I even finish uttering the word, here she goes again:

"And do you have any children?"

"No," I say.

And I sit silently. For a moment, she feels uneasy. Only for a moment. And this is my only, small satisfaction.

When I was younger, I used to get the following variety of replies:

"There's still time, there'll be children, God willing!"

"Oh, you're still young, all you need to do is drink catkins tea. I have a girlfriend who couldn't have children for ten years and she drank catkins tea, and after only a month she was pregnant. Her son is already in school now!"

"You know, it's better not to have children right away. A person should experience other things first. Mature parents are the best parents."

Now it's different. I say no, and they only make that compassionate face. Like: I'm so sorry. What can you do? It's not your fault. Not everyone can show pictures and baby teeth. Someone has to stay outside this circle.

The girl combing my hair is convinced that she will be in this circle. She hasn't the slightest inkling that there may not be a place reserved for her fairy-tale story over there. At seventeen, she thinks that by the time she reaches forty she will have had plenty of time to do all the things she ever wanted. She doesn't even want to consider the possibility of waking up one day as a middle-aged woman, alone and with varicose veins.

"Close your eyes and try to imagine the following scene: On your right there are only women, and on your left, men. There is an empty space between them… do you see them? Do you have an idea what they're like, what they look like, what they do?"

I saw them. Quite clearly. It was the first picture that came to me, as stupid as all the other first pictures that come to me while talking here with her, but I had no alternative but to admit:

"The women. They're like those ancient statues, wearing togas, or whatever those dresses are called, the ones worn over one shoulder. Their hair is gathered up in a bun. They're beautiful, tall, they seem proud, some are holding jugs and, all in all, they don't move around very much. They look like they're posing. They're smiling. They're timeless. Their beauty is everlasting. I know they spent a long time making themselves pretty for this scene, spreading scented oils on their bodies, bathing in special spas and fussing for a long, long time over their perfect hairdos. Their dresses are in gentle pastel colors, pale pink, peach, these dresses almost blend in with the color

of their skin, something like that... they have long, perfect arms...."

"And the men?"

"They have their backs to me, almost all of them. They're terribly obsessed with their work and worries. They're wearing dark suits. They look, I guess, like people from the present. But I don't see any of their faces. Only the backs, collars, ties, glasses, a lot of hand motion, folders and papers being moved from one hand to the other, a kind of undefined murmur among them, some sort of haste, but not cheerful... they're not aware of the women standing across from them. They don't even know they exist. But even if they did know, it wouldn't matter because they're doing something that is much more important."

She had this sad look on her face. And it's no wonder. I too would have that same sad expression on my face if anyone were to tell me this.

"What would you say to these women? Is there something you would like to let them know?"

"Hmmm... I would tell them... you're very beautiful. I'm in total awe of your beauty. And I envy you. I would like to be like you."

"Really?" she asked, "why would you want to be like them?"

"No, actually, I would like to look like them, but on the other hand, I would still want my life to have some meaning. They're only there to look pretty. I need something more."

I knew this was bullshit. At first I blurted out, in haste, something I truly believe. Or something I thought I was supposed to believe. Or something someone once told me I had to believe. Damn it! I know what she's trying to say. She's trying to say that this is an ideal image of a woman I picked up as a child from my mother. I'm familiar with the babble.

"All right. Is there anything you'd like to say to those men?"

I'd prefer not to. Really. Not to them, or anyone else for that matter. That's what I wanted to say to her. But this was not an option. This hour had to be endured regardless of the amount of humiliation it entailed.

"I don't know.... I'd tell them they were boring in those suits of theirs. And that they should take a look around, look up from those piles of paper."

But this was also bogus. Everything was bogus. And I no longer knew how to get out of it. I'm not lying to her. I'm not even lying to myself. It's more complicated than that. Someone else is lying to me and forcing me to lie. It's not true that I think men are only interested in work. Why then did I arrange this scene in such a way? Why?

"Look at me," she said, and I realized I had lowered my head practically between my knees and that I was holding my face with my fists. "At what point did you switch roles with your mother? When did you start worrying about her?"

"Why do you think we switched roles?"

"Remember the small and the big elephant. . . ."

"I remember the elephants."

"When did it happen?"

"Who knows, probably a long time ago. I worried about her health. I worried about whether she would find a job. We would go together to look for a job for her. She was sick a lot. I would visit her at the hospital. But these things happen to everyone. It's not something she could have avoided."

"Correct. But maybe she shouldn't have allowed you, as the child, to worry about such things?"

"It was difficult for her. When she divorced my father, there were so many things to worry about. Then that man came along and, I guess, for her he represented some sort of a solution. But, he didn't like me. And he didn't want me in his house. And so I stayed there only for a short time. Shorter than planned. . . ."

"I know. We talked about that."

"I know we did. You're the one taking me back to it."

"No, I wasn't taking you back to that."

I didn't say anything. A sadness, completely different from anything I had ever felt before, began to rise within me. I could see my mother's face suddenly withdrawing from me at an inconceivable speed, and had I done what I really wanted to do at that moment, I would have probably run over there, after that face. But I remained seated. And the face continued to withdraw. Until it became a little dot in my mind's eye.

"All right," I said, "I know I'm not exactly her dream come true. I know that. I'm not, in any way whatsoever. But there's nothing I can do to fix that."

"And how do you feel knowing you're not her dream come true?"

"Above all, it makes me sad. Why can't I be her dream come true? What's wrong with me? What I mean to say is, there must be something in me that could make a mother proud?"

"And what else?"

"It also makes me angry. Because I know she would never, ever, even under torture, admit to the things I'm saying to you now. She would never admit that I'm a complete disappointment to her. She would say it was all in my head. She would say

she was very proud of the things I've accomplished in my life. But, you see, it's like this: her entire being emits 'I don't like you and I know you realize I don't like you, but till my dying day I'll act as though I don't know that you know, because this way I'm punishing you even more.' Something like that. I don't know if you can follow me."

She just nodded. She was following me. And how? I always knew exactly when she was following me. I continued:

"Not long ago, I tried an experiment on her. She had reupholstered her sofa and chairs, choosing a new color. I came to her place. As soon as I entered the door, she asked me if I liked it. I didn't really, but that wasn't important. In any other situation I would have said it was okay. Because, if she liked it, then it was really all the same to me, do you understand? That's what people expect from us: when they buy new shoes or a new dress, all you should say is that it's great. These are the little white lies that make life easier. But, she never did this with me. She never liked the things I chose. She was always certain I wouldn't make the right choice, unless she was there to shop with me. She only liked the things she chose herself. And that's why, when she asked me about the sofa and chairs, I suddenly got the urge to say what I really thought. I said: 'Listen, I'm not too thrilled about the color, but if you like it, that's fine. This is your home and it's important that you like it.' You should have seen the expression on her face! She was

so offended! She was so shocked! For the rest of the afternoon, all she did was talk about it, making me rethink my opinion again, and again, and again, so that I might come to the conclusion that I do like her sofa and chairs after all. And when I still wouldn't admit that I liked them, she became openly aggressive and said that, in her opinion, burgundy is a morbid color for an apartment. And you should know that many of the things in my apartment are burgundy, no less. There you go… just once, just once I did what she had been doing all her life and she couldn't stand it."

Outside, someone was persistently trying to start his or her car. I know a lot about cars. That's probably one more thing my mother wouldn't approve of. I knew what was wrong by the sound it was making. I recognized the whrrr, followed by a click, and then nothing; I wanted to shout to the guy outside that the problem was in the starter, and that he needed to replace the brushes, and in the meantime, if he wanted to start the car, that he should bang on the starter with some kind of a rod, really hard, so that the brushes come in contact with what they're supposed come in contact with and strike a spark.

"What's happening?" she asked. "Why are you so quiet?"

"I'm tired. Suddenly, I'm extremely tired."

Then I told her how I met this girl who was adopted and how, for some reason, I feel terribly sorry for her.

"Why?"

"What do you mean, why?! Her real parents simply abandoned her when she was just a baby and she lived in a hospital for a year, until some other people came to take her. And do you know what she does now? Let's say the two of us are driving somewhere and she says she needs to stop and buy some cigarettes. Before getting out of the car, she always says, as if joking: 'You'll wait for me? You won't leave, will you?' The first few times she said this, I didn't react. But then, on one occasion, I stopped her and said very seriously: 'I won't leave and I won't abandon you. I don't abandon people.'"

"Like they abandoned you?"

This was a low blow. We were talking about someone else, not me.

"Who abandoned me?"

"Your mother abandoned you," she said softly, but very clearly.

There was no mistake about it. I didn't misunderstand her or anything like that.

"Why do you think that?"

"You told me yourself. Between that man and you, she picked him."

There was nothing more to be said here. I knew, better than she did, that it was the truth. And still, I was as surprised as if I'd been told I was the one who was adopted, and not that other girl. As if I'd suddenly been told I was an alien, or something like that.

See what's ahead of me now? Years and years and years. During which I'll know she had abandoned me. Dinners during which I'll know she had abandoned me. Birthdays during which I'll know she had abandoned me. Conversations during which I'll be pretending I didn't know she had abandoned me. Or, will I pretend to be bad at hiding the fact that I know she had abandoned me? Which one of us will be better at pretending that we don't know what we know? And how long could this go on?

I could've cried, of course. That's something a person can always do. But somehow, I feel like this now also falls under the repertoire of those bogus things that had lost their meaning. Only a week ago, I thought I knew how things stood, roughly, anyway, and now, I'm back to knowing nothing, without hope of ever finding out. I didn't have any time left to ask her anything, and besides, I think the question would be too complicated for this period of the day. In other words, if I've been fed lies all my life, if I answered with lies, and if everything in my life up to now was a lie, then damn it, do I even have anything sincere to offer?

I know exactly what she would say. "Is that your real question or are you asking something else?"

Shit! At one time, I was the one who liked to relativize things.

EIGHT

Better that you hear it from me now than later, from one of them. I'll look like I was hiding something, as if it were something important. I think they exaggerated and made too much of it.

Anyway, it has to do with the time I didn't speak for almost three months. All right, maybe it was closer to four months. But no longer than that.

It all started out as a joke one evening while we were playing cards at home with our friends. However, no one knows that during a card game, I also play that little gambling game with myself. For example, I say to myself: if I lose, in the next five days I'll get hit by a bus while crossing the street. And then, naturally, I fight for my life. No one really wants to be hit by a bus.

I was winning almost to the very end. That was when the game took an amazing turn and my husband was dealt a really good hand. I covered my eyes. They laughed and cracked numerous cruel jokes at my expense. People can be unusually cruel during a card game. They're capable of sending you to your death. Of course, they were convinced that I would soon raise my head and suggest a rematch, or that I would offer them a cold beverage. But, as far as I was concerned, there wasn't going to be any more talking. I have nothing to say to people who don't value my life whatsoever. That's understandable, right?

They tried everything to make me laugh. At first, they even had a tiny chance of succeeding. I remember having to make a small effort not to laugh and focusing on my own gloomy thoughts, in order to remain in the same position. My hands over my eyes. Elbows on the table. Their giggles, which were slowly turning into boredom. If only they would forget about me, I thought.

After a little while our friends got up to leave.

"Are you going to see us out?" they asked.

It still seemed like a good joke, the silence.

They left and I didn't budge an inch. Good manners suddenly didn't seem important anymore.

During the next few hours, my husband tried everything he could think of to get me to talk. He tried to win me over by being sweet, hugging me, making funny faces, dancing the Kazachok, marching in front of me; then he became angry, and again went back to being nice, but the grip of silence only grew stronger. I thought: Why can't a person decide to be silent for once? Why is that so unusual?

And so we went to bed without me uttering a single word. I did all my usual evening chores in silence. I did the dishes, watered the flowers, turned down the bed, removed my make-up, showered, disconnected the phone, set the alarm clock, and got into bed.

I fell asleep in an instant, like someone who has been sleeping on their feet for some time, only they weren't permitted to rest their head on the pillow. It was a good night's sleep, without dreams, without waking up, without nightmares. It was the kind of sleep I used to have as a child, when I wasn't troubled by all the things I needed to do the next day. I wasn't ready to fully admit it to myself at the time, but somewhere deep within I knew: I wasn't going to do anything tomorrow. Except for the things

I need to do for myself and the things I find absolutely pleasing.

The next day, my husband woke up before me, which was out of the ordinary. I heard running water in the bathroom, and then he opened the refrigerator, made tea, took a cup from the cupboard and for a little while longer made all these usual morning sounds which were, I guess, supposed to wake me up. But, I was already awake and perfectly aware of the fact that I didn't want to get up and that I didn't want to go to work. Besides, who really wants to do that? Such things are done mechanically, because we have to, and not because this is something we want to do. On the contrary, I wanted him to leave for work so that I could slowly get out of bed and take a walk by the river. I wanted to be quiet and to think, and the fact that the very thing I considered to be perfectly normal was being made out to be extraordinarily odd, made me determined to finally start behaving as I see fit. This was one of those moments of unusual clarity of thought that comes early in the morning. That is to say, all my life I've wanted only two things: to be completely passive and to be silent. Of course, I always did the complete opposite of this, so much so that there were years during which I would completely forget about what I wanted. But this morning, everything came back to me, appearing in our window in the form of a perfectly clear, blue sky. It was one of those idyllic spring days. A perfect day, I thought, for starting a new life in which I will no longer make an effort to do anything.

My husband, however, didn't see things in the same light. Not on that morning, at least. First, he began calling to me from the kitchen, and then he came into the bedroom, stood by the bed I was lying in and, a little annoyed, announced the time.

This information meant nothing to me. I knew I wouldn't be going to work. Not that day, nor any day in the future. Never, in fact. I didn't like it, the morning rush through the traffic lights, the climb up the stairs, the faces waiting for me at the office, that cluster of meaningless papers and the pile of unpleasant news. No. I will no longer have any part of it. Watching the sky is much nicer, I said to myself.

He simply couldn't believe that I didn't want to get up. He brought me tea, sat on the bed, and for the first time, looked at me with real worry.

"Are you ill?" he asked.

He touched my forehead. Then he looked at his watch, and at me again.

"What do you want me to do?"

He rested his head on my chest. I was sorry he didn't understand. I caressed his hair.

"Tell me what's wrong. Please."

He sat there for a few minutes, with his head on my chest, his hand on mine, and I almost hoped that he would join me, that we would doze off together, untouched by the outside world. But then he looked at his watch again.

"Is it that time of the month? Is that what's wrong?"

He got up, wavering, and then finally said:

"All right, I'm going to work now and you try to get it out of your system. I'll call you as soon as I get there."

The days that followed could have been even better if the people around me hadn't been so intent on making me talk. It didn't matter that I did all the usual chores, went shopping for groceries, cooked dinner, brushed my hair, dusted. Each morning, after my husband left for work, I would go to the park, carrying a book.

Sometimes, I would sit in the park crocheting a curtain and watching the children play. They could have been wonderful spring days if only they had let me be.

To them, all these very normal human activities weren't proof enough that I was living and that I existed. My mother came over every day. She would sit by me and cry. I would crochet in my sofa chair, or watch a movie on television, or read, do the things all ordinary women in the world do, and she would stare at me and cry. I would be peeling potatoes or carrots and she would be choking with tears next to me, as if I were already dead and buried. It seemed like refusing to talk was the cruelest thing you could do to your loved ones.

This was so strange to me and completely beyond my comprehension, and I didn't know how to help them. Silence had descended upon me as though it was the most natural thing in the world, and to me, the more they tried to pull me out of it, the more they became unusual and estranged.

One day, they brought home a doctor who took my pulse, listened to my heart, and examined my pupils. He waved some little lamp in front of me and moved his forefinger from side to side. He too tried talking to me, but his words didn't even enter my range of hearing. My mind was able to separate, better than ever before, the important from the unimportant, people I should hear from those who mean nothing to me.

"We'll put you on sick-leave," said my husband after the doctor had left, "or else you'll lose your job."

As if that was even important.

For a little while after, it seemed like they understood. My mother came over regularly and she didn't cry anymore, nor did she try to talk to me. Sometimes she would just sit next to me and hold my hand. She would give me a kiss on the forehead, then my cheek, and then quickly turn away.

My husband still spoke around the house sometimes, but that too was becoming less frequent. Our life slowly took on a new form, the way people adapt to all new situations. One night, he cautiously moved his hand towards me, not knowing whether this silence also meant that we weren't going to be making love. But, of course, silence was just silence and nothing more. It wasn't aimed against anyone. Even silence can endure a hug.

After that night, we began making love again, in silence and in a slightly different way than before. But, to some extent, our bodies were closer than ever. It was just our flesh and us. And a deep silence in which we swayed back and forth.

During those days, I thought I had finally found a good

way to live. I'll crochet many curtains, read many books, scrub my stove until it sparkles, bake the most unusual cakes, and no one will ask me unpleasant questions.

Friends gradually stopped coming over, and to my great relief, my world was reduced to a very small circle of people. The doctor, however, still came to see me from time to time. He would listen to my heart and then go into the other room and whisper something to my mother and my husband.

It seemed like my life was going quite well. I read novels, dictionaries, and cook books with equal passion. Now, in the silence, words revealed their full beauty, and thoughts, the thousands of thoughts that lay wasting away on our shelves for years, suddenly revealed their full meaning. I could see the people who, in their silence, wrote these books hoping that someone, in some other silence, would read them. I could sense when their thoughts faltered, and when the passion of writing seized them with ease and then carried them through the next few pages.

One afternoon, however, the doctor came, bringing with him some sort of an injection. For weeks now, he had been treating me as if I were some kind of an object and not a human being, even though he wasn't willing to admit to it. He sat next me, opened a metal box, filled the syringe, and placed my arm on his lap. For an instant, I thought about pulling my arm away, but that would be the end of my passiveness. And I enjoyed it so much. So, I left my arm there, to see what would happen.

Without even looking into my eyes, he took a ball of cotton, rubbed the part of my skin where the vein appeared and stuck me with the needle.

It was only then that he looked at me. He didn't say anything, but I could clearly see the triumph in his eyes: "You wanted silence. Now you shall have it."

This, of course, was a contemptible way for them to cut short what was one of the most wonderful periods of my life. For some reason, which I definitely can't seem to comprehend, they consider you normal only if you live contrary to all your needs. And this is what they demonstrated to me, towards the end of that summer, in a banal, obvious, and rather brutal manner. The people I believed loved me. I thought they understood and that they would never force me to do anything I didn't want to do. I thought they would allow me to live my life with the intensity and pace that suited me. Instead, they tricked me and brought me this doctor and his needle, after which silence lost its beauty and meaning.

It wasn't the same after that. And I was no longer in the place I wanted to be, but more and more in a hazy hospital room in which the silence was constantly interrupted by someone's screams, sobs, the sound of tapping heels, screeching wheels, sirens outside the windows, early morning chatter of cleaning ladies who displayed their conviction that I was but a mere object, even more than that doctor. While changing my sheets, puffing my pillow, pulling me up, they would continue the conversation they began in the previous room, then open the windows and leave without even glancing at me, happy there was only one more room left at the end of the corridor.

This no longer resembled what I wanted. I didn't like the solutions they were offering. I could have stayed in this room and let them give me those injections. I could have gotten up and tried to escape, but then I would no longer be just a woman who didn't talk, but a fugitive from the hospital. And finally, I started talking again.

"I'm so happy," my mother said, her eyes filled with tears. "I'm so happy you're well again."

“I’m happy too,” I said.

Happiness. So, from now on, this is what we’re going to call the deception we would continue to live in. We’ll end my sick leave and start from the beginning.

As we all hugged with excitement and while they were telling me how much they missed me, their eyes were sending me a message: Don’t you try to escape from all the shit or we’ll drown you in it. We talked and talked and talked, like people who hadn’t seen each other in a long time.

NINE

Even prior to this, I wasn't really in the habit of talking to anyone about the thoughts that sometimes come over me. But after this experience, which my family euphemistically calls "my episode," I have absolutely no intention of sharing any of it with anyone. People simply don't want to hear about such things, no matter how much you think they love you. In reality, they love what they believe you to be or what you should be. And if sometimes you point out to them, even in a subtle way, that you might be something else, maybe just a little different from the way they perceive you, they become disappointed, frightened, worried, and angry. They feel that what you want to be is not safe for you. Only they know which way of life is safe for you. And your safety is much more important to them than your wish to exist in your own authentic form. Who today can allow themselves the luxury of being completely unique and completely relaxed? And so, if you're well-mannered, or if you don't have the strength to quarrel, you simply give up. Just like I gave up.

This is why they will never get to know anything about my thoughts. And for this, they'll be secretly grateful to me because they simply wouldn't know what to do with them.

I'm convinced that the people who love you are the last people in the world who would want to know your true feelings and thoughts. If you don't believe me, try letting them know some of these things, and you'll see. You'll be faced with unbelievable problems.

The more they love you, the less they want to know the true you. It goes so far that they don't even want to know what you did during the day. They want you to tell them a pleasant and carefree lie. If you love them, you will do just that. After all, why would you upset them, why would you dissuade them from believing that you're finally safe? What would be the benefit of that?

Honesty is entirely overrated. People swear by their

honesty as if they were talking about some special kind of honor. Thereby forgetting that honesty equals cowardice, unless it's a form of aggression.

If I were honest, everyone who loves me would have to leave me. Or I would have to leave them. So tell me, what's so great about honesty? And who among you has only good thoughts, those that wouldn't bring any of your loved ones into a state of absolute panic?

Suppose my husband asks me how my day was. And suppose I start my story with what happened that morning. I was crossing the street and when, in the midst of a crowd of people racing to make the green light, I suddenly thought that I was going to start screaming for no apparent reason. I could barely resist the urge. I could easily picture myself: I'm crossing the street, only halfway, and then suddenly I come to a halt, take my sunglasses off (don't ask me to give you a rational explanation for these details because I haven't one) and as I stand there bare-faced, gazing up towards the sky, I begin to scream. I scream and scream, and the people stop in astonishment, looking around, a crowd begins to form on the crosswalk, the traffic light turns red, but the street is still filled with people, looking at me, frightened or shocked, the drivers are honking their horns, some are even trying to make their way through the crowd who is listening to my screaming in disbelief.

Sometimes I think I won't be able to resist the urge. And the bigger the crowd, the stronger my urge becomes – to do something completely inappropriate.

So, I tell him about that morning. And then I continue to tell him about how I was going down the stairs and how, like numerous times before, I imagined myself falling down those stairs and somewhere along the way, breaking my front teeth. Not my back, not my head, arms or legs, not any of that, only my front teeth. They all get chipped and look horrifyingly hideous, while I lie at the bottom of the stairs, contorted and beaten up.

Why would anyone want to listen to such things? People want you to tell them about things that are interesting, to give them a recap of a movie you had seen, they want to hear a piece of juicy gossip or how good they look and how they've lost weight.

Imagine if I then tell him how at 2:15 p.m., as usual, I watched Edgar as he went to work. Edgar looked sluggish, as if he didn't get enough sleep. Something was stuck to his shoe and he shook it off. Edgar's bus came on time.

After I see Edgar off to work, I have another half an hour or so and then I head for home.

On the way, I fantasize about how handy it would be to have a lover somewhere halfway between work and home. I would tell the cabdriver to wait for me outside the apartment building. All right, he can turn the motor off, but leave the meter running. I think I'd even like knowing the meter was running while I'm committing adultery. This somehow illustrates the true state of things. Your meter is always running anyway.

I take my panties off while still in the elevator.

There, in that apartment, the blinds are half drawn, it's quiet and everything is ready for my arrival. He's sitting in a chair, naked. Everything is ready for me, get it? I throw one shoe off in the hallway and the other in the room. By the time I get to him, I've taken off the necessary items. We don't say anything; I straddle him in his chair. At first, we don't move very much. It's more like we're feeling each other from the inside. He nibbles at my shoulder. Takes me with both hands. Rocks me back and forth. I squeeze him from within....

If now you tell me that this seems detached, I could agree with you and advocate the theory that sex in general is a category of alienation, or if I decide to be really stubborn, I could defend the argument that two united bodies can never be detached because the connection is the point of the union. How much you draw from this connection, these two energies, is another matter. Don't blame it on the silence in the room of my imaginary lover. In any case, I can get carried away defending either one of these theories, no matter how different they are. No matter what you think about it, it's all the same to me. And because I don't have a firm opinion on the matter. Sometimes I honestly believe sex cannot be detached. Other times, I think it's always like that. But most of all, I think such discussions are totally stupid.

Let's go back to my lover and me; we are now really going at it in the chair. He lives on one of the top floors, because as I'm hugging him around the shoulders, behind him, through the blinds, I can catch a glimpse of the contours of other high-story buildings, and over there, in the distance, I can also see a river. The only sound in the room is the occasional clanking of streetcars. And the sound of us breathing. There is no music to sweeten or jazz up the event. Music is forbidden. As well as smiles. Or a comfortable bed. Anything that might soften this image is strictly forbidden.

His face is mature and tense. His cheek is scratching my shoulders. Occasionally he bites hard into my shoulder. If it hurts too much, I clench my teeth. We're both in a hurry. We know the meter is running and that I have to get home soon. And so we pick up the pace. One strong clench at the end, a tiny cry from me or from him, a moment of silence and stillness, and then I'm already getting up and gathering my clothes off the floor.

As I'm putting on my shoes and leaving, he slowly gets up, lights up a cigarette, and goes to the window. Maybe he's watching me leave, or not. I've never stood at any of his windows and I don't know where they're facing. And that's why I don't know if he can see me as I get into the cab and continue my ride. I always have a feeling he can, but it's also very likely I'm wrong. In fact, he might be looking in a completely different direction, forgetting about me as soon as I close the door. Which is okay in a way.

The cab driver is waiting for me downstairs. He's reading the newspaper, smoking a cigarette, not suspecting a thing. He says: All done, madam, finished? I say: Finished. He asks: Where to now? And I give him my address.

We drive on. That good feeling between my legs lasts a long time after.

It would be nice to have a lover like that. And then to come home and lie back in your tub, your sofa chair, your bed. Wash up, change into something comfortable, heat up some soup. And talk about the insignificant things that happened that day. I think this would make the usual everyday house chores even more pleasant. I can distance myself enough to see this scene played out. My husband and I are sitting at the table and blowing into our spoons of hot soup, I'm smiling at him the way every woman should smile at her husband during dinner, making the usual chit-chat like please-hand-me-the-salt and would-you-like-some-more-soup and what's-on-TV-tonight and I-could-really-use-a-nap-now-what-about-you and here's-half-the-newspaper, and everyone is happy.

Later, I felt like she already knew so much about me that it was becoming unbearable. I wanted to never see her again. I wanted to crawl into a hole and hide somewhere far from everyone. Most of all, I wanted to hide from her.

It started out harmlessly enough: By relaxing my body, from the tip of my head, down my neck, then through my lungs… the light that was supposed to pass through me and nurture me. That's what she said. "Observe the thing that is your life… find the vulnerable, painful places and nurture yourself…."

All I could see was endless space, very similar to the photographs of the universe. Everything I wanted to touch seemed too far to reach. Standing between me and everything else was an immense, never-ending darkness. For some reason, this was what my life looked like at that moment, and it slid from the top of my head towards my feet in this exact form. Millions of tons of darkness, remoteness, implosions, and black holes descended through me. And when she said my feet should sprout roots, it was quite unnecessary. The black holes had already riveted me to the ground with a force more powerful than anything she could possibly say. And so I sat there, with roots coming out of my shoes, eyes closed, and hands crossed in my lap.

"Go back to your earliest childhood," she said. "Imagine you're watching an unedited movie. Various images appear. They're not in chronological order. Some images are nice and others not so much. There are both happy and sad images. Some linger, while others just fly by. Try to see yourself in all these images. . . ."

One image appeared immediately, but it wasn't important. Many other images followed. Shadows on curtains, at night. My grandfather reading me a bed-time story. Grass. Worms under a rock, and their bodies wriggling on a little branch. Screams of other children as I fling a worm at them. A well in the middle of an orchard. My grandmother yelling at me not to go near the well. Me, going there anyway, as soon as no one is looking. A look down. The coldness it emanates. The taste of the water in the bucket. Water that makes your teeth go numb. The smell of the fence. Grandfather's tools for painting the fence. Cans. Brushes. Paint thinner. Garage. Old court documents grandfather refused to throw out. My mother is brushing her hair in front of a mirror. Her underskirt, showing a little under her dress because that was the fashion. The two of us are watering flowers. We're adding a little ink to the water to make the hydrangea blue. We're shaking a tree and apricots are falling down on us. They're very ripe and unbelievably sweet.

"...now, out of all the images, try singling out only one and then focus on it."

For no apparent reason, the image that wasn't important at all kept coming back to me.

"If one of the images keeps popping up persistently while you're chasing it away, then maybe you need to devote your attention to it...."

How the hell does she know exactly what's happening? Where did she learn to do this?

I gave in. All the other images were disappearing anyway, like in a whirlwind, before this one image. Small, meaningless, insignificant.

"When the image becomes clear and when you come to see yourself in it, along with all the other important elements, you may slowly open your eyes. When you're ready...."

I'm not ready. But, sooner or later, I have to open my eyes. That's when I'll start crying. This was becoming increasingly absurd.

"Welcome," she said with a little smile when I opened my eyes and looked at her.

And then she gave me some paper and coloring pencils, just like she would a child. So, we're going to draw again. I was long pass the tolerable limit of self-humiliation, and so I simply began to draw the scene, as my tears fell on the paper and turned my drawing into some sort of an infantile aquarelle.

"All right," she said when I completed my idiotic drawing. "Give the picture a name. And take a good look at it. Go inside of it."

I'm in the picture, damn it. What else do you want from me? She didn't have any tissues. She brought me a roll of toilet paper. So, there I was, sitting, with a roll of toilet paper in one hand and the drawing in the other. Can a grown person be in a more humiliating position?

"Tell me what's in the drawing."

"This is our hallway. There's only one suitcase in it. Here, on the right, is the door. That's it."

"Where are you in the drawing?"

"I'm not in it. I'm everywhere and nowhere. I'm like some kind of a ghost."

"Draw it."

I drew myself in a cloud, like in one of those comic strips.

"Whose suitcase is it?"

"My mother packed the suitcase, she's a school teacher and she

has to take her students on a field trip. I'm six or seven years old and I'm devastated because she's leaving."

"What's the small red thing on the suitcase?"

"It's a poem I wrote. I put it on my mother's suitcase and I'm hoping she'll notice it when she goes to leave."

"What's the poem about?"

"Some sad children," I said.

But I lied. I remember only too well that the poem was about some dead children. I couldn't say it out loud. I thought it would sound too insane.

"So, you're in this house like some ghost and you're looking at the suitcase which is making it very clear what is to follow."

"Yes, the suitcase doesn't leave any room for hope. There's nothing to be done."

"There's nothing to be done," she repeated after me, nodding her head.

As if she wanted me to hear some of my sentences again. As if sometimes she wanted to make sure she heard me right.

"So, you're looking at the suitcase and... What does it look like? If it could talk, what would it say?"

Whatever, if the elephants and the membrane around the baby could talk, why wouldn't the suitcase? Nothing seemed strange to me anymore.

"The suitcase is a bit uneasy and annoyed, and it says: 'Why is this kid circling around me? I'm here on a sacred mission to protect the ironed dresses. I can't be a responsible suitcase while kids stomp on me. There's no way. You can't expect that much from a suitcase, even if it is the strongest suitcase of all, like me! Besides, this kid is getting on my nerves.'"

"So, the suitcase feels no compassion whatsoever for the child?"

"Well... it does, actually, but its duty comes first. The suitcase can't allow its emotions to get the better of it because this would have a negative effect on its performance. To the suitcase, the dresses it holds inside are the most important things in the world. When it reaches its destination, everything must look perfect."

"Does anyone in the house notice what the child is feeling?"

"No, no one. Maybe just the door."

"What is the door like?"

"Old and wise. It has seen so much, but it's powerless to do anything. The door has seen things no one else has."

She was silent for a while. She was thinking, I guess, whether or not to ask.

"What has the door seen?"

I took a few more strips from the roll of toilet paper. Everything was so surreal. The spring afternoon, the voices in the street, me sitting in a nice wicker chair, the woman sitting across from me, listening to me talk about what the suitcase and the door were saying as if it was the most normal thing in the world. I couldn't help but observe this scene from the outside as well, the entire time. This made me feel even sadder. I saw myself, a pathetic, desperate, middle-aged woman, sitting there and crying over something that was meaningless, something that happened ages ago.

"The door saw this child kneeling a few times on the door mat, out of fear."

"Did the child kneel anywhere else, or was it just in that one place?"

"Just there. In front of the door. Several times."

"Is there, someone who senses what the child is feeling?"

"There is. My grandfather. And nobody else."

"And now? What's the situation now? Who takes care of this child now?"

I didn't have to think twice.

"My husband," I said. "He's the one who takes care of me."

"And do you think you do the same for him?"

"No. I neglect him. My attention is directed towards other things and other people, least of all him. I sometimes feel guilty because of this."

"And in the meantime, life goes by," she said, in a manner which wasn't quite like her.

It occurred to me that she might have recognized something from her own life.

We both looked at the clock. My time was running out. It was time for me to wipe my tears and walk out of there all bloated from crying. Giving me time to slowly return to normal, she continued:

"You have very strong abandonment issues. It's as if you're in constant fear of being abandoned. You know, I found the games I too played in my life very interesting and later, I analyzed them. Maybe your game is to compensate for your fear of abandonment by abandoning others…."

If only you knew, I thought to myself, how appealing the idea of abandonment is! To leave everything behind and go live on a mountain. To leave everything and live in sin somewhere where it's warm and where the wind is soft. To radically change your life, take a new name and live on some other continent. To abandon yourself. Above all, yourself. To be carefree, beautiful, new, and young in someone else's skin! If you only knew....

TEN

Luka? Let's see what someone named Luka is doing in this chat room. I click on his name twice.

"Hi, baby. Busy?"

"Hi. No, not really."

"Quite a familiar name."

"Is it?"

"Yeah. Very. Where are you from, Luka?"

"Belgrade, Serbia."

"No kidding?"

"Nope."

"Well, Luka, I think I have a surprise for you."

"Surprise me, baby...."

"No need for your English anymore, sweetie."

"WOW!"

"Wow is right! Belgrade online as well."

"Oh, great!!! I've never met anyone here before from our parts! Phenomenal! To be honest, I was getting tired of the English."

"How old are you Luka?"

"Twenty-five."

"Oh, still a baby."

"What about you, Lucy?"

"Hmmm, a little older than you, I'm afraid."

"Go ahead, tell me. I'm not into young girls anyway."

"No? What's wrong with their tight asses and perky breasts?"

"Listen, young girls usually have no idea what they want. It's all an act. They're immature."

"And you're not like that? You're not immature?"

"I think I'm different from most of them."

"Oh, Luka, we all think that about ourselves. That we're unique."

"Tell me how old you are, please."

"Forty-three."

"Wonderful! A real woman…."

"You think?"

"Oh, yeah. I watch them sometimes in the streets, or in the streetcars; they're aware of their beauty, but they're really good at hiding it. Know what I mean? They don't need to look for their reflection in every store window like the girls."

"Are you sure you're only twenty-five?"

"I swear."

I take a quick glance at the corner of the screen. 5:24 p.m. He could come home at any minute. I should take the lasagna out of the freezer.

"Luka, I've gotta get going soon…."

"Oh… too bad. You visit this chat room often?"

"Well, sometimes. When I find time."

"When will you find time again?"

I think I hear the elevator. No. It's going to another floor. It's not him yet. But it will be soon.

"Lucy? You still there?"

"I'm here, Luka. Just thinking."

"Lucy, what about tonight?"

"I really don't know."

His cough syrup is sitting there, next to the keyboard. He's been coughing for the last two weeks. Wheezing. I would get a scorching bristly ball in my throat every time I think about his cough. Or anything else that might happen to him.

I get up to open the window. There's too much smoke in here. Then I glance at the screen again. Luka isn't writing anything. He's waiting.

“Luka?”

“I’m here, Lucy.”

“Luka, can you chat tomorrow night at 10:30?”

“All right. I’ll be here.”

“Okay. Bye. I’ve gotta run now.”

“Wait! Just one more question! You married?”

“Aha.”

“Okay. Talk to you tomorrow. Be good.”

“Get lost!”

As I leave the chat room, a few ads for similar links pop up on the screen. Lick me – says a big-busted blonde with her finger in the right place. Eat my WET WET WET pussy – is written on the leg of an incredibly long-legged, dark-skinned beauty. My eyes linger a few moments longer on the area where those extremely long legs flow into the torso, take a deep breath and I turn off the computer.

Lasagna. It’s time for me to finally heat up the lasagna. Do we have any ketchup? He won’t eat it without ketchup.

No matter where we start, the two of us always go back to something that hurts. Or used to hurt. Or I'm afraid might hurt.

"This is getting too humiliating for me," I tell her. "I'm constantly whining. This can't be. I'm not like that."

"Like what?"

"It can't be that I'm someone who constantly complains."

"I find that you have an unusual expression on your face when you talk about the things that hurt you...."

"What do you mean?"

"You smile. You're constantly smiling."

"Unless I'm crying."

"Yes," she says laughing, "unless you're crying. Why do you smile when you talk about serious matters?"

I can't believe she's asking me this! Did I wander into the wrong office?

"A smile doesn't always have to mean a person is in a good mood. A smile is also a matter of politeness. You can also smile at a funeral when someone is expressing their condolences."

She's nodding her head, but she doesn't seem quite convinced. I go on to prove my point:

"Who knows why women smile. There can be so many reasons. They might want to charm the person they're talking to and engage them in a conversation. By smiling, we let the other person know we're willingly participating in the conversation. All right, I agree that a smile can also be a defense mechanism. But you smile as well!"

She ignores this and says:

"Can you try to pay attention to your facial expression while you speak, for a short time at least? To allow your face to express your true feelings?"

"Are you trying to say that my face doesn't show what I'm really feeling?"

"I didn't say that. I just said that sometimes you smile when you talk about very serious and painful matters. How can the person you're talking to know what you're really feeling if you're smiling?"

What is she doing? What is she trying to tell me? That I always hide my pain, or that my "pain" is, in fact, bogus and that my face is giving me away? Which of the two is she referring to? I don't ask.

In any case, she won't be getting anymore of my smiles today. It seems best for all concerned if I just sit in my chair and cry. This way, I appear more like the patient, she appears more like the therapist, and everyone's happy.

That said, she goes on to another fabrication:

"Do you remember a fairy tale which meant a lot to you as a child?"

Hey! I know this game! Now I'm supposed to say something based on which you're going to interpret my perception of life! This all too typical question makes me want to scream. Besides, I wanted to tell her, all fairy tales are designed to make me look like an idiot. Which one should I choose? Cinderella? That won't do, after all, I was an only child. Sleeping Beauty? Right, then I'd have to listen to her tell me how I've been waiting all my life for a prince to come and wake me from my everlasting dream with his kiss. Indeed, which fairy tale did I like?

"This won't work," I say to her. "The problem is I know the reason why you're asking me this and I can't think of one."

"You don't want to expose yourself?"

And then the smile again. Aha! Go ahead, smile. Meanwhile, you've banned mine.

"Truth be told, I know now, from this perspective, where this exercise is going. But back then, when I was just a child choosing a story I liked the most, I didn't know this. So, I think it makes sense to mention the fairy tale my grandfather used to read to me at bedtime…."

"So then, there is that one story?"

"Yes, of course. But it's almost pointless talking about it. It's extremely obvious."

"Never mind. Tell me."

And then I told her the story about a boy who lost his parents and wandered around the world trying to find them again. Somewhere along the way, he came across an old man and they continued the journey together. They travelled halfway across the world, got into various predicaments and dangerous situations, and in the end, due to a lot of luck and practically a miracle, the boy managed to find his parents.

"Is there any need for me to interpret this for you?" she asks.

She's finally beginning to understand.

"No, really no. I told you it was obvious. But, nevertheless, this was a fairy tale from my childhood. And who knows how

many times my grandfather had to read it to me…."

"What does that story remind you of now?"

Our two heads on an enormous down pillow. His soft voice. His irremediable Russian accent. I see him reading the story and falling asleep in the middle of a sentence. I'd nudge him a little with my hand and he would awake with a jerk and continue reading. This is how we would lull each other to sleep, only he never nudged me once I dozed off.

"It reminds me of my grandfather," I say.

"What was your grandfather like with you?"

How do I explain this to her? I wanted to say that he was the love of my life.

"He always had time for me. Lots of patience. He would let me write on his typewriter. We would go to the Russian library together and read newspapers. We liked similar things. We would go on boats and tour the city from the river. We would go to the movies. We would tell each other all kinds of stories… basically, we had a wonderful time when we were together."

She's going to make me cry again. And yet, I'll feel bad about it when I get home. I even put mascara on, intentionally, to prevent myself from crying. But it looks like it's not going to stop me.

"So, what message was he sending through his actions? What was he letting you know by doing all these things with you?"

The message was: "I love you," that's what he was letting me know.

"Well… the message was probably: 'I have all the time in the world for you, I enjoy your company.'"

"We could also say the message was: 'You matter.' Right?"

"I guess…."

And here go the tears again. An outrageous amount of tears. She says:

"Let it all out. Don't keep anything back."

And I let it out, but only to a degree. She sits silently for a while, and then she asks me when my grandfather died and where I was when it happened.

"I was twenty-five at the time, and I was by his side when he died. It was a solemn experience and it was a good thing I was with him at the time."

I told her everything, wiping my tears the whole time. I also told her I didn't cry at all, not then, nor later at my grandfather's funeral. The tears came later. I told her how I let go of my grandfather's hand when I realized the end had come, so as not to disturb him in his passing. And how I looked up, thinking his soul was already somewhere on the ceiling, looking at me from above, suddenly confused and frightened, not knowing what was happening to it. And how in my mind I tried to comfort and calm the soul on the ceiling by whispering to it that it's all right, and that now it will slowly go into the light.

"So, you can accept other people's weaknesses. You know how to conduct yourself with people, even during their most difficult moments. Why can't you accept your own weakness? Why does it make you angry?"

I'm silent. I have no more strength left to answer her questions.

"What would your grandfather say about your occasional display of weakness?"

"He would probably say I inherited it from all those Russians and that it's something I should be proud of. That would be so like him. . . ."

"But still. . . ?"

"But still, whenever we talk like this, I can't help but observe the two of us from the outside, from a different perspective, and to me, all this seems so dreadfully pitiful and pathetic. It's like there's always someone else sitting here, in this other chair, mocking everything I say."

"And what is this other person sitting here saying?"

"They're saying I'm pathetic. And immature."

"What would this critic's message be?"

"The message would be: 'Grow up already, it's high time!'"

"If I asked you what star you were born under, what would your answer be?"

"I wasn't born under any star. I was born under the Moon."

"And what is the Moon like?"

"Melancholic."

Her eyes were telling me: "There you go. There is no cure for you. It's just the way you were born."

And then, who knows why, she brought up the question of trust. Do I trust her? I told her I entered into this with honest intentions and that, sometimes, I might be playing a kind of game, in which case I'm not purposely deceiving only her, I'm also deceiving myself.

"Do you think I have any doubts concerning your honesty?" she asked.

"No, not at all," I said, and I truly meant it. "I think you know I'm being completely honest."

And then, out of the blue, she felt the need to state her conclusion. I liked her specifically because she didn't make any big conclusions, and now, suddenly… just like that, she told me to think about whether I opened up to her in my own pace. Could it be that I opened up too much and too quickly? Is this something I usually do? Do I establish trust that quickly in other situations as well?

No, no, no, I wanted to scream at her, don't do this to me, you yourself asked me if I trusted you, and now this is turning into a nightmare. Why are you doing this? I don't understand. And then, as if she wanted to finish me off, on my way out, she told me I had this need for a happy ending. Where did she get that idea? Oh yes, from the fairy tale I told her.

"That's not true at all," I was picking up pieces of my self-respect, along with my purse, cigarettes, sunglasses. "It's been a long time since I had any illusions about a happy ending. What sort of happy ending can one expect if everyone dies in the end anyway?"

She was smiling, and I could tell she didn't believe me. She had already placed me in a drawer where she keeps all those hopelessly waiting for a happy ending. And there was no changing her mind.

It occurred to me later, because I always remember what I should have said after the fact, that absolutely every fairy tale had a happy ending. Besides, what's so terrible about expecting a happy ending? A part of me knows I'll die, sooner or later. Another part of me still hopes for the fairy tale happy ending. Is that any reason for her to knock me down on the way out!? Or am I supposed to learn something from this?

Even if that was the case, I still wasn't getting it. I was just getting more and more angry with her.

This is why this is the perfect time for me to tell you something I didn't want to mention before because I didn't want you to think I was a nit-picker, but now I don't care anymore. After our second or third session, I forgot my sunglasses on the end table in her office. I realized this as soon as I left the building, but the next patient was already inside, and I couldn't go back and interrupt them. So I decided to send her a text message. A very simple message: "I forgot my sunglasses in your office. Please keep them for me until next week."

So did she answer back?

You're right. She didn't.

What did she think? That she would get involved in something that goes outside the boundaries of a patient/therapist relationship if she replied to a simple text message? Or maybe she thought I intentionally forgot the sunglasses in order to take our relationship to a level that was not acceptable?

There's something demeaning about that, if you really think about it.

Next week, my glasses were waiting for me exactly where I had left them, but I never forgave her for not replying to my message. And I never will. This doesn't mean I didn't consider the possibility that maybe, subconsciously, I did leave them there on purpose. See what they're capable of doing to us.

ELEVEN

I'm at the door, leaving. My husband is touching my face.

"Your cheeks are so hot!" he says.

Then he slides his hand down to my neck.

"And your neck is cold. That's odd. A flushed face and a cold neck."

What do I tell him now? Nothing. A kiss. Quickly, a kiss. That always helps. And a smile. My best smile. Maybe I should caress his balls? Would that be too much? Of course it wouldn't. I always do that. I'll do it again now. Don't be paranoid. Easy. Easy. A few more seconds and you'll be out the door.

"You better watch out when you get back," he says as he places his hand over mine, while I gently stroke his balls through his pants.

And he gives me a devilish smile.

Some green monsters from outer space are scattering across the TV screen behind him.

Outside, I'm greeted by science-fiction fog. I am breathing loudly through my mouth.

This fog is suffocating me. I'm old. Meanwhile, I'm hurrying off on a date with a boy. If someone happened to attack me in this fog, I wouldn't even be able to run. I'd choose to stay there, and die.

I listen to my steps on the damp pavement.

I'll never get to the cab stand. He's probably already coming after me. But even if he is, I wouldn't be able to see him in the fog. That's just stupid. Of course he's not following me. He'd never run outside in his sweat pants. He won't even go to the corner store dressed like that. There's no way. I've gone out at night like this a hundred times in the past. A thousand times. And nothing. There's nothing different about tonight as far as he's concerned.

And intuition? What about intuition? Men have no intuition. Women do. The hell they do. They're the last to find out their husbands are cheating on them. Such intuition doesn't exist. It's something we only read about in books.

I turn to look behind me in the dark. No one's there. No one's there. Just a few more steps. I get into a cab.

So, this is what it looks like. I'm on my way to meet the boy I met in the dirty chat room. And it's quite clear we're going to make love tonight. Why else would we be meeting in an apartment? What if my husband is in a cab behind me? What if he's following me? Dear God, this is so absurd. He'll leave me. There's no doubt about that. To risk losing everything for one fuck. Don't think about that. Think happy thoughts. Prepare yourself. Think about the eyes of that young man. Gazing at you. Over there in the darkness. The way he moaned when I moved my hand across his back....

Suddenly I feel a mild spasm, somewhere in the pit of my stomach. I lean my head against the headrest. I realize my fingers hurt from gripping onto my purse so tightly. I ask the driver:

"May I light a cigarette?"

And then I gaze at the streets and buildings and traffic lights going by. The city looks absolutely eerie in the fog. I look at my watch.

Five more minutes and I'll be there. A kiss at the door. Or are we going to be all embarrassed again? The hell with embarrassment.

And what if the cab driver goes back to the same cab stand and my husband, who was of course following me, approaches him and asks where he took that flustered woman? Maybe he'll even discreetly place a bill in his hand for this information, just like in the movies. Do cab drivers have some sort of honor code that restricts them from giving out such information? Should I perhaps warn him of this possibility and remind him that he mustn't tell? That he should be vague and say something like: "I took her downtown…"? No way. I can't tell him that. He'll think I'm crazy. He'll know exactly where I'm going. I'll look ridiculous if I tell him something like that. Besides, no one is following me. Turn around. Discreetly. See. There's no one there. The hell there isn't. He's there somewhere. It's foggy. I can't see a thing. Finally, here's the building. Pay the driver. Should I nevertheless warn him on the way out? Nonsense. Don't make a fool out of yourself. Step out of the cab. Calmly. As you would normally. Look behind you. No one's there. The street is completely empty. One, two, three… third floor. Lights. He's waiting for me. That handsome boy is waiting just for me. Go on… smell your collar. Nice perfume. Go on. The elevator. The mirror in the elevator. Everything is fine. I have dark circles under my eyes. So what? I also had them when I was twenty. The lips are fine. The eyes are a little tired, but other than that, they're okay. The perfume, the perfume is the most important thing. Great perfume. We're stopping. Stop staring in the mirror and get out of the elevator! Should I knock or ring the doorbell? Knocking would be silly, sort of old-fashioned and conspiratorial. Nor will I cheerfully ring three times. I'm not cheerful. I'm terrified. One short ring. Oh, God. He's going to open the door now. Oh, my God….

At the last second, I remembered. I scratched at the door with my nails.

That's how you go to your lover….

I smile at the thought of this.

This is how he finds me. With this smile on my face. And my hand in the air.

A little later. We're already drinking our third shot of vodka. Things are beginning to look much better. The boy is simply sitting at the kitchen table, across from me, gazing at me with his hand under his chin. Once in a while, he raises an eyebrow and softly says:

"What...?"

As if he managed to hear a part of what I was thinking about, but not too clearly.

I reply:

"Nothing...."

Or I don't say anything at all. I just look at him.

I'm thinking it's a shame I can't go anywhere outside this apartment with him. It would be nice to show him off to my girlfriends. What a perverse thought: I'd like it if my husband could see him! Sitting here, like this, and gazing at me with that almost lovesick look on his face. How great would it be if he could see this! You idiot. You stupid, stupid, stupid idiot. You're not doing all this out of vanity, are you? This boy is much too beautiful to be used only to feed your vanity. The vodka is excellent. What does that perpetual reply of mine mean anyway? I don't drink. Grow up! Adults sometimes drink when they're having a good time. Or when they're sad. Or tense. You have the right to do the same. Why not?

"You look sleepy," says the boy.

"I'm just a little tipsy."

"That's not bad," he smiles.

"No. Not at all."

He's sitting very close to me now, hugging my legs with his knees. I occasionally run my hand across his face. Nice drunken fatigue. Blissful indifference.

Fingers, fingers, fingers….

The boy softly trembles under my fingers. Surrendering completely.

All right then, I think to myself, let me show you what I've learned in the meantime, while you were still learning to read and write….

"You've wiped me out," says the boy after a considerable amount of time, very softly, while putting his head down on the pillow.

His muscles were still trembling a little, as if stricken with fever.

I start laughing:

"I thought you were going to wipe me out!"

"And I will, as soon as I recover."

Later, in the cab, the boy whispers to me:

"Will you be online tonight?"

"Why? So that I could tell you how it was?"

"Of course," he says and gives me a little kiss on the neck.

His hand is still somewhere between my knees. The cab is racing. Empty streets. An even denser fog than before. The boy is then silent for a while, his gaze turned away from me.

So, it's started. I already need him to look at me, and he's turning away.

"You're lucky," I whisper. "No one is going to ask you anything when you get home. You don't have to face anyone right away, the second you enter the door."

As soon as I said this, I realized how stupid it was. He doesn't know what I'm talking about. He's only twenty-five years old; he's never been married and knows nothing about it. He doesn't care that I have to go back home now and ring the doorbell. What if my husband really did follow me?

"You can do it," says the boy.

Suddenly I feel this anger building up inside of me.

Easy, easy. He's just a kid. He's trying to say something to make you feel better. He doesn't know that what he said sounds inappropriate.

As I walk from the cab to my building, I feel a surge of completely irrational fear. I'm almost racing, barely able to catch my breath in the fog. I feel like I'm going to suffocate before I even reach the apartment.

I stop before entering the building. I'm trying to calm my breathing. Then, I think about crossing myself.

Why in the world would God help people like me?

Nevertheless, I quickly make the sign of the cross and press the elevator button.

In the elevator, I look at myself in the mirror again.

Where is the woman who was racing off on a date a little while ago? This one looks tired and shaken up. Anyone could tell a mile away what you were doing all evening. You reek of alcohol. Wait… in the pocket, look in the pocket… here it is… a mint. Put your lipstick on. That's right. But not too much. If you put too much on, it'll look too obvious.

I undo my scarf and examine my neck and shoulders in the mirror.

Thank God, there are no visible marks. But my skin is slightly red and inflamed. Damn it, it's not as if he's going to examine me through a magnifying glass. Calm down. Go straight for the bathroom as soon as you go in. Make a fuss about something. Dear God, it's almost midnight. So what? You've come home later than that numerous times. Yes, but with a clear conscience. My panties are completely wet. What if he hugs me at the door? Of course he won't. He's stopped doing that long ago....

He opens the door for me.

How did he look at me?

"Oh, what a horrible night," I say in a rush, looking away, throwing my purse on the chair. "Have you had anything to eat?"

"Yeah, I made French toast," he says, like a proud child.

There you go, stupid, you've ruined your fun for nothing. The man was making French toast while you were going crazy with fear.

"It's awful outside?" he asks.

"Terrible. Can't see six inches ahead through the fog."

"How did you get back?"

"I took a cab, of course. I'm off to take a shower, I feel the soot of the city on my skin."

"Do you want me to make you a sandwich? Are you hungry?"

"That'll be great!" I shout from the bathroom, now feeling at ease, knowing I'd been saved this time and that everything went well. "And put on some tea, will you?"

"Okay, hon!" my husband shouts back from the kitchen. "We'll get you warmed up in no time."

TWELVE

Some things can never be forgotten. Certain scents. The morning you woke up feeling the perfection of life in your still very young body. My right profile in the bathroom mirror of our family home. When I stood up in the tub and leaned just a tiny bit forward, I was able to see my right profile and my wet hair clinging to my head, as well as a part of my right breast which, back then, stood firmly in an enviable position. I liked the shape of my nose. I felt like it embodied a kind of softness, which, no doubt, people find attractive.

I remember the small box of glue my grandfather used. A plastic box with a small round section for the plastic spatula. We don't use things like that today. Now we have tubes, scotch tape, staplers. No one uses ordinary glue anymore to attach two pieces of paper. It takes too much time. I remember the smell of the glue and the firmness of the plastic spatula and the little lumps the glue made on the paper, which we then needed to spread around using the spatula. Back then, it seemed like we had our whole lives ahead of us. And everything was in a kind of a calm state of joyous anticipation. Now I know: that was it. That was the moment of beauty. Nothing this beautiful ever happened again.

My grandmother used to dry her own mint and basil on top of armoires. She would place newspapers on top of all the armoires, as well as the guest-room beds, and there she would spread the fragrant herbs. I remember the pleasant chill of those rooms and how the half-dried mint crackled between our fingers and crumbled on the newspapers when we touched it. I remember how opening doors made the newspapers rustle, and disturbed the dry herbs. We walked slowly through these rooms so as not to disturb the drying process. We spoke in hushed voices so that our breaths wouldn't lift up the newspapers. To keep everything from flying to the floor, we would close the door before opening a window. We all waited until my grandmother slowly and very carefully gathered the herbs from the newspapers and stored them in linen bags, specially sewed for this purpose. Later, we would drink mint tea, which smelled better than anything ever before, and cured us of all ailments.

In another room, my aunt sometimes dried walnuts. While still green, she would place the walnuts on the floor and wait for the hull to dry and fall off.

Many years later, when we sold our house, this was the last thing I saw before leaving those rooms forever: a few green walnuts drying on the wood floor. No one wanted to take them. They were left there, a few walnuts in an empty room. This is also something I will never forget. Though I would prefer to forget because of the pain I feel every time I remember. Nice memories are better. And I always think: What did the people who came to live there do with the few walnuts they got with the house? Did they throw them away? Did they put them somewhere and wait for them to dry, and then eat them while thinking about us? It's much more likely they simply swept them up with an ordinary broom and threw them away.

I remember the big cold pantry that led to the attic. Shelves. And hundreds of jars with labels on them. I remember my aunt's handwriting - the sharp, slanted, almost masculine numbers she wrote on the labels, to mark the year, and then glued onto the jars. Such things don't exist today, or maybe I don't know they exist, those small jar labels with zigzag edges, similar to stamps. On the walls, pots and pans of various sizes used to hang from cords.

And then, there's my first typewriter, which had its own cleaning kit under the lid. Cleaning the typewriter was a process filled with various pleasures. I would remove the black build-up from the small holes of every letter, and then clean the needle. Slowly, letter by letter. First the capital letters, then the small letters, and finally the numbers and punctuation. Then, it was time for the brush. It would remove everything the needle left behind. And then, the final moment of pleasure: putting in a sheet of paper and trying it out. The typed letters were clear, clean, and legible.

If you wanted to destroy me today, all you would have to do is place one of these items in front of me: a small box of glue, a typewriter cleaning kit, a drying walnut, jar labels.... If you really wanted to finish me off, this would be enough.

I was still angry with her when I went in for my session the following week. On the drive there, I practiced what I was going to say to her: the words I was going to use, and the tone. I tried to anticipate her reaction.

I brought up those three things.

The smile on my face when I talk about difficult matters.

The way I open up to others. And her question as to whether I opened up to her in my own natural pace.

And finally, the part about expecting a happy ending. I told her no one in his right mind expects to end up in an oncologist's office or some ditch somewhere. We all somehow hope we'll find peace and as much contentment as could be expected in our old age. But, we all also know that a fairy tale ending is just an illusion and nothing more.

"It's not fair," I said, "for you to label me as someone who naïvely expects a happy ending based only on the ending of a fairy tale I told you."

However, she turned most of her attention to the other part.

The part about opening up.

"Why did that comment upset you so much? I just asked you a question, a simple question: 'Did you open up to me at your usual pace?'"

Why can't she understand? This is not a natural situation and the natural pace cannot be applied here!

"Don't you understand," I asked, "how much this question can shake a person's will? You may very likely discourage a person from ever coming back to therapy after a question like that! Therapy is, presumably, just that - a process through which a person is supposed to open up. You have witnessed the amount of humiliation I had to go through in order to completely expose my thoughts and feelings. And then, after all that, you tell me I opened up too much. And, what's worse, that I might be doing the same thing in my everyday life!"

"I wasn't judging you. I asked you so many different questions, why is this one such a problem?"

"Because it's vital. You can't all of a sudden say I turned out to be naïve because I trusted you. Not after this long process of establishing trust!"

I also wanted to remind her of the soft voice she used to relax my body, the way she made me draw stupid things from my childhood and then cry over them, as she assured me there was no reason to feel shame and that it was all perfectly normal. I wanted to tell her about how she tried to convince me to believe the pillow was, in fact, the baby from my dream and how I had to play the roles of the membrane and the big elephant and the small elephant, and that it was all her idea, not mine! And now, all of sudden, it turns out I opened up too much!

"That's not what I said."

"But that's what it sounded like."

"All right. I realize I hurt your feelings with my question. What I wanted to say was: Did you open up because you were following your nature or because you thought it was something you should do? I don't want you to open up only because you think you should, if it's something you don't usually do."

What is she trying to say? That I'm really an obedient child, a goody-goody who'd been told: "Now you're in therapy and here you have to expose your feelings to the bone, no matter how much it hurts?" Could it be that all that crying earlier brought her to this conclusion?

"Okay," I said, "but then you should have said so, instead of creating a misunderstanding."

"What does that critic of yours say to all this, the one from our last session? What does he say about the way you've opened up?"

"He doesn't say anything."

"And about me?"

"Well... he says that you're improvising. I disrupted your plan for today's session by talking about this, and now we're out of time, so you're trying to come up with a way we can spend the remaining twenty minutes or so."

She laughed:

"That's partly true. But it's also important that we discuss the feelings you came in with today. How do you usually express anger?"

Ha! Ask my husband, he'll tell you. He can also show you the scar on his forehead, if you're that curious.

"With explosive, short-lived outbursts. I get over it very quickly, unless it's something really big. But the fact that I don't know how to forgive someone who really hurt me is a much bigger problem. I realized some time ago that forgiveness is one big deception of Christianity. At least in my case."

"Which person in your life couldn't you forgive?"

"You already know. I told you about it. But this has nothing to do with that story."

She made that face of hers, 'I know everything and I can sympathize with anything,' and said:

"This has nothing to do with me, this anger you're feeling."

Well, now she made me really angry!

"Of course it does. I can do you a favor, if that'll make it easier for you, and tell you it's really projected anger against my father, mother, a former lover, or whoever, but it wouldn't be the truth. This is exclusively your doing. Don't tell me you're incapable of making a mistake?"

"What is on the other side of your anger?"

Sometimes, she really confuses me with her cross-examination. Really, what is the opposite of anger?

"Well, I guess some kind of passiveness, an inability to fight back."

"May I say that you're very sensitive?"

"Of course you may. I'd even feel better if you did."

"Why?"

"I always thought of myself as being more sensitive than most people, but then it occurred to me that this kind of thinking might be overly narcissistic. Everyone is sensitive in their own way. But, if you also think I'm sensitive, in a way that confirms my assumption…."

"Well then, from now on, I'll have to watch what I'm saying to avoid hurting your feelings."

"No, you don't. That would put a strain on you. You can say whatever you like, but allow me the right to react in accordance with my feelings. Like now, for example."

"Of course you're entitled to that. In fact, therapy is a combination of mutual understanding and confrontation. Going through these two processes leads to authenticity. But... you mentioned most people. How do you see yourself compared to most people?"

"With regard to what?"

"Anything."

"You can't generalize. I'm average in some things, in others above average, and still others below average. I really can't answer that question."

"Yes, that's a fair and reasonable answer. But, if you observe yourself as a whole, couldn't you say whether you were above or below average, or just average?"

"You're forcing me again to say something I'll feel bad about later. All right, if we're talking about things that are important to me, if we're talking about spiritual growth, I think I'm a little above average, but for God's sake, people don't say things like that out loud and why are you making me do it!?"

She clasped her hands in her lap. Here come the conclusions.

"You see, we've been talking about your anger for almost an hour and you can't find it in yourself to forgive me."

"That's not true. There's nothing to forgive here. I don't doubt your good intentions. This is more of an intellectual problem, which I wanted to discuss with you, than anger. You called it anger."

"Nevertheless, you can't forgive me… and this sets a new boundary between us."

Could it be that this was hard on her?

"What are you doing now?" I asked. "Am I supposed leave here with a guilty conscience as well?"

"Of course not," she laughed. "However, if it bothers you that you have problems with forgiveness, we can work on that."

"Well, it might be good to let go of some of my anger. It's a little absurd to be angry with someone all your life because of something that happened long ago. It's a heavy load to bear."

"I agree."

Then she said something and I got over my anger in an instant, if I ever really was angry with her:

"If I were your friend, I would now be able to engage in this conversation in a very different manner, meet you head-on

and play the power game a little. However, since I'm your therapist, this confrontation is very precious to me."

Aha! So I see! You could knock me down if it weren't for the code of ethics. You could easily beat me if you wanted to.

"If your goal was to remove my mask of excessive politeness, then you have certainly succeeded," I said on the way out.

"Do you think it's off now?"

"Good God! I've taken off only one of them. This is only the beginning...."

THIRTEEN

Something truly incredible happened!

I tuned into Baltimore at 2:10 in the afternoon, like I do every day, expecting Edgar to show up. And he did, at 2:15 as usual. He stood at the bus stop with his briefcase in hand, like he always does. He was wearing the blue jacket I've grown accustomed to. Underneath it, I saw the dark blue pullover I also knew well.

Then suddenly, Edgar turned around for the first time, and looked straight at me! He was really looking at the camera, but it was just as if he was looking at me. First he turned around, but then, it appeared as though he realized there was a camera there, moved toward it a step or two and looked up. For an instant, our eyes met. Edgar smiled. He really smiled. He stood there for a while longer examining the object holding up the camera. This was the first time I was able to actually see his face. I had an uneasy feeling that he could see me as well, that he literally knew I was sitting here, watching him as he waited for the bus. Edgar was looking right at me and then, he scratched his head. He smiled into the camera again and then looked around worried, I guess, that somebody might see what he was doing. So, Edgar also does crazy things when he thinks nobody's watching!? Aha!

At that moment, his bus arrived. Edgar moved toward the front door of the bus and, just when I thought it was over, when his figure was already in the bus, for only a split second, I saw Edgar secretly waving his fingers behind his back. And that was that. The bus was gone.

Edgar was probably just playing around. Or not. Or he assumed that there was a good chance someone was watching him at that moment, considering the enormous number of maniacs sitting at their computers. So he waved and smiled. To whoever. But why today? Why to me?

I stopped believing in coincidences long ago. I think there is a sequence of events that leads us from one point to another. In our inability to control this journey, we call it coincidence. But, of course, there is no such thing as a coincidence.

You could say it was nothing more than a coincidence when, one day, fifteen years ago, I lost my scarf on the 16e bus that ran from Zeleni Venac to Block 45. I got off before the last bus stop when I suddenly realized I didn't have my scarf, and it wasn't just any scarf. My mother bought it in Rome, and after having to talk her into loaning it to me, I lost it. No, that was unacceptable. I ran like crazy in-between the buildings to the last stop because I knew the bus would be parked there for a while before starting off again on its route. When I got there, the bus was already starting to leave and I threw myself in front of it, forcing it to stop. I ran in and the scarf was there. Meanwhile, I was completely out of breath so I sat down thinking, all right, I'll just ride the bus for a while until I catch my breath and then I'll get off. That's when I realized there was a young man sitting in the seat next to me. Don't worry. I won't drag on. To cut the story short: the young man sitting there, is my husband. Now you tell me if there's such a thing as a coincidence. Was it a coincidence that I ran the way I did, that the scarf slid off my shoulders as if, at some point, it came alive and decided to go a separate way; that it was the last stop, when the bus driver takes his break, giving me enough time to catch up? I don't think so...

there's also the other part of the story, his part. He got on the wrong bus. He wasn't familiar with this part of the city. So when he realized his mistake, he decided to ride the bus to the last stop and then go back and transfer onto the right bus in another part of the city. He says he saw me while I was still wearing the scarf. But I didn't even look at him. Didn't even notice him. Then, I got off the bus and he noticed the scarf lying on the floor next to my seat. He says that he just stared at the scarf in anticipation. He didn't know what he was waiting for, but he waited. And when I rushed into the bus again, he knew he had been given a second chance. Or the first and only. Because there's no such thing as a coincidence.

This is why I have to see what's so important about this day, the day Edgar finally looked into the camera, smiled at me, and waved.

For breakfast, I had cheese and crackers with hot chocolate.

I started the car on the first try.

I stopped at a crosswalk to let an old woman cross the street and thought I was being not only civilized, but also generous. It wasn't as if I had to stop. She looked at me, I gestured with my hand for her to go, she looked at me one more time, as if she wanted to make sure we were in agreement, and then started crossing the street apprehensively. Needless to say, another driver was already behind me, impatiently honking his horn. But I was enjoying the fact that the old woman was walking slowly and that I had a perfectly good reason for annoying him. I waited for her to step onto the other curb before I continued driving, slowly and without hurrying.

What else happened today, before 2:15? Did I tell you? I work in a travel agency. People come in, tell me where they would like to go, I check to see if there are any available seats and then sell them the plane tickets. Or I make reservations for them on flights of their choice. It's mostly a pleasant job. All you have to do is search the computer. And answer the phone. Yes, it gets hectic at times. Most people travel during the holidays and in the summertime. That's when it gets difficult to convince them that there are no more available seats on the flights going to the seaside. But, for the most part, it's a laid-back job.

Anyway, a man came in today who happened to be looking for a plane ticket to Baltimore. I usually don't even look up, and even if I do, I don't think I could give you a description afterwards. If the police ever came to ask me to describe the man who came in that morning at 9:15 to buy a ticket to Paris, like in the movies, I wouldn't be able to tell them if he was twenty or fifty years old, tall or short, bald or with a baseball cap on his head, if he was wearing glasses or had a mustache. They all look the same to me, if you know what I mean. They tell me what they want, and I check in the computer and write out the tickets.

But I looked at this man, because he said he was going to Baltimore. I paused and looked at him. He was a little over fifty, slightly overweight, wore an expensive suit, had grayish sideburns, and a sweaty forehead. He's probably going there on business, I thought to myself. The only unusual thing about him was his eyes. Very dark and very focused.

"Baltimore?" I asked.

"Yes, Baltimore," said the man, still gazing at me with those eyes.

"Why are going to Baltimore?"

"It's my turn," he said.

"Is it true that it's always raining in Baltimore?"

"That's a lie, of course. Just like everything else you're going to hear about Baltimore from other people. Someone else's impressions have nothing to do with the way you experience things."

"Do you know Edgar?"

"As you well know, Edgar is a big loner. No one can say they really know Edgar. You probably have the best chance of getting to know him."

"What do you mean by that?"

"Nothing. I'm in a hurry. Sell me the ticket so I can go."

No. We didn't have this conversation. Or did we? I'm not completely sure anymore. We could have had this conversation had it not been for those two women hanging over my head and babbling about yesterday's game show in which someone almost became rich. I just sold him the ticket to Baltimore, via Munich, and after neatly placing the change in his expensive crocodile leather wallet, he left.

It was after this that Edgar looked into the camera and smiled at me. Coincidence? I think not.

FOURTEEN

As I was getting out of bed that morning, as I waited for the water in the tea kettle to come to a boil, as I watched the shadows dance through the curtains in an attempt to touch the spice jars which irretrievably shy away from them each morning, I thought to myself: I could grow old soon and at some point, when it's too late to do anything about it, discover that I did everything wrong.

This would imply a few things. First of all, that there is a right and a wrong way. Then, that we are the ones who decide which one of these ways is going to take the shape of what we call our life. And furthermore, this implies the existence of exclusivism in the relation between the right and the wrong way. On the other hand, maybe these two ways are a mixture of both right and wrong?

I tried to find comfort in this as I drank my tea, but the fear was still there. I couldn't dispose of it like I did with the bag of Earl Grey. It just stood there, soaking and turning black. It wasn't something you could sweeten. Dilute with milk. Or decide not to drink. Fear seized my morning in an all too familiar way: it appears unexpectedly, somewhere in the pit of my stomach, making my insides tremble, then it slowly rises up my diaphragm to my chest, causing my heart to stop for a second, only to demonstrate the extent of its power, and just when I begin to think it has finished me off, it races to my throat and starts choking me.

"All right," I said to my fear. "What do you want from me? Where are the two of us going this morning?"

My fear stood silent, staring at me. It loved to establish a hierarchy for the day, first thing in the morning. It had to let me know what is most important. And who is in charge. After we settle this, it allows me to make decisions concerning the less important things. It is only interested in the strategic set up. For example: will I live through another day?

What if I realize, on the last day of my life, that I stayed in the wrong place when I should have moved on? What if something was waiting for me in a place I didn't feel like going? What if everything could have been different and infinitely better had I remembered the right sentence at the right moment, the only possible answer to the posed question? What if I didn't turn around when I should have, and missed something that had been intended only for me?

There are times when you know your life is really yours and you feel like you completely belong there. However, there are those times when you clearly know it's just one of the numerous lives you could have had. And all these other lives suddenly begin to sting like newly acquired blisters.

"Are you trying to tell me," I asked my fear, "that I have a certain obligation to these other lives I basically know nothing about?"

My fear was smiling at me slyly, tilting its head to one side, shrugging its shoulders, pretending to be someone who let's me draw my own conclusions, make my own decisions, handle things the way I see fit... what a snake! An outsider might even get the notion that I actually had a choice!

She told me to imagine a cliff - a sharp, isolated cliff looking over the sea. I wanted to tell her I actually stood on a cliff like that once, in Northern Ireland, and that it wasn't a bit romantic. All I could think of, there on that cliff, was how easy it would be to throw myself down on the sharp rocks and into the icy cold, surly water.

All right then, a cliff. Any cliff. And a view of the line where the sea meets the sky in the far distance. And my hands, slowly transforming into wings. Totally absurd, but I went along. I never had wings in my dreams about flying. I always flew using only my arms. So, I'm flying, flying, flying and I see an island. And what else could possibly appear in the middle of a sea? If you ask me, the island is covered with sharp rocks, rocks no one would ever wish to land on. But, she told me to land. First, I feel gravel under my feet, then stones, grass, and finally soil. This surprised me. I didn't expect grass. At least that's not what it looked like from above. And then a forest. A thick forest overflowing with shadows. Our lives are made up of mundane places, so much so that it makes me sick. Cliffs, wide-open spaces of the sea, forests full of shadows… nevertheless, I continue to walk in my mind through this forest of cheap symbolism, and I feel very uneasy. I don't have much of an adventurous spirit. At least not when it comes to venturing alone through a forest full of shadows. On a deserted island, no less. Although, no one said the island was deserted, but I guess it's implied. Life observed from above, from a cliff and then across the sea, can't help but resemble a deserted island. My thoughts are wandering, and that's not good. I should focus on the trail in front of me, which of course winds through tall trees. What are these trees supposed to be? My life goals? My failures? My fears? Diseases I'm going to be stricken with? Orgasms? It's not important. Anyway, I'm walking through this forest and – you guessed it – I come across a house. She doesn't tell me what the house is like, but I see a pleasant, wooden house. It's got a porch with two or three steps leading up to it. It looks like a house out of a Western movie. I approach the house and tune into my feelings. Curiosity, but not too much. Absence of fear. Almost like performing a duty. The house is there. You have to go into the house. That's it. Nothing spectacular, nothing that would indicate a major revelation.

I'm opening the door. At first, I don't see anything. My eyes are getting used to the darkness. What do I see in the room? Indeed, what? Slowly, I start to make out shapes. A wooden table in the middle, chairs set up around it. A piano on the left. Closed, dusty. No one is playing it. A rifle is leaning against the wall in the corner. Am I going to tell her about the rifle? Who knows how she's going to interpret that.

Her voice is guiding me on, it says look to the other side, there's a figure standing there and you're amazed to discover it looks just like you! What's it made of? What's it like? Look carefully, stand in front of it, see if it has anything to say to you, face it. . . .

I wouldn't mind seeing Barbie standing there. We were born the same year; she wouldn't have anything against playing my double on a deserted island. But, it wasn't Barbie. The figure was made of dark wood. It was uneven and warm. It had something like a veil over its head and face, it was holding a baby in its arms, which was also wooden and uneven and, all in all, it looked like a character from a mural. Like Virgin Mary. Instead of feet, the figure had a pedestal. I could clearly see it had no feet. I stood in front of it, and the figure looked at me and said, "Why are you so cold?" And that was it.

Later, I returned down the same boring trail through the forest, across the beach and the sea, to the same cliff I started from.

"When you feel that your arms are no longer wings and when everything returns to normal, you can slowly open your eyes," she said.

My arms never did become wings, and things are never going to be normal, so I opened my eyes right away.

I told her about my double from the island.

She led me to the middle of the room, shoved a pillow in my arms and said I was now the wooden figure without feet. The pillow was, of course, my wooden baby.

"How do I feel in that house, on that deserted island?"

"Peaceful. Good. I'm performing my duty."

"What is my duty?"

"To raise this child and then let it go across the sea, then to the cliff, and from there, into the world."

"Am I lonely there?"

"A little, but at the same time I know I'm fulfilling my sacred duty as a woman."

"What do you think about your visitor from the cliff?"

"She looks a lot like me, but at the same time, she's very different. She wouldn't be able to spend her life here."

The tears were very close, on the very edge of my eyelids, but amazingly, this time I held them back. There's no use crying over a wooden woman without feet, which only could have been me. I made a conscious decision not to be her, I kept repeating to myself.

Later, back in my chair, I told her, trying to convince myself first, and then her as well, how I always felt disdain for this archetype, according to which women become saints the moment they fulfill their assigned womanly duties.

"It's important for you to understand that both these characters are a part of you. The one over there, and the one here. Maybe you don't like the one over there, maybe it frightens you that her feet were changed into a pedestal, maybe that means she has a strong foundation, or that she can't budge from where she's standing, but whatever the reason, she represents some part of you. This is something you have to accept."

"She's so ordinary," I said. "She thinks she's a saint. She has that serene look in her eyes full of silent reproach for any woman who ever wanted to be anything other than a woman."

"But she's still a part of you."

"And what did she mean when she said I was cold? I don't see myself as a cold person at all!"

"What could that coldness be?"

"She is under the illusion of being eternal. She thinks, only because she has procreated, that she has made herself eternal.

Unlike her, I live every day with the knowledge that I'm disappearing. Maybe she sensed I was aware of my fleeting existence and interpreted this as coldness. Women like her think very highly of duration, of passing their boring, monotonous existence from one generation to another, with as little change as possible. There's something narcissistic about this, if you ask me. Parenthood in general is a type of socially acceptable narcissism. Every parent dreams of bringing into this world his own clone, and then adding the finishing touches he himself is lacking."

At the end, as if reading me a bedtime story, she told me some story from her area of expertise about how damaging it is not to accept every last part of your inner self. About how, if you bury yourself in only one of these characters, sooner or later, you fall into the state I am in now.

So now it looks like I have to make room for the Lady Saint. The fact that she never existed isn't important, what's important is that I acknowledge the fact that she could have existed. Something like that.

Her wooden child opened its eyes and looked at me. I already told you I'm not good with children, even when they're made of wood, even when they're mine, from one of my other conceivable lives.

Its wooden eyes rested on me and it slowly stretched out its little wooden hand towards my cheek. Lady Saint stood still, satisfied, peaceful, as if she wanted to say: "There, you see!" For a second, I thought she was going to thrust her wooden child into my arms, for me to hold it a little. But, I didn't move my arms and the wooden child didn't manage to touch me, because I didn't budge an inch. I just stood there, looking at the two of them and thinking how this was only one of those cliffs one could take a leap from. Who knows who I would find waiting for me on some other island?

FIFTEEN

All I did was accidentally bump into that stupid CD shelf, which was standing in the wrong place anyway, making it difficult to go out on the terrace without making at least some contact. My husband didn't say anything special. He just yelled, "Be careful!" But his tone was offensive. You know what I mean? As if I were someone who always bumps into things, and intentionally turns over and breaks his CD's.

There are days when I don't even notice such things.

Then again, there are those other days when something like this is enough to make me start an argument, which then lasts for hours.

You guessed it. This was one of those other days.

That's how it started, slowly but surely, leading to the moment when we're both in bed, because it's already late, and we've already argued in the living room and the kitchen; gone through our round of insults from the bathroom to the bedroom, as he turned down the bed and I removed my make-up; already managed to release the introductory poisonous arrows, which guarantee a night of quality sleeplessness, and now, here we were in a bed, wide enough for each of us to wrap ourselves up tightly in our own blankets and avoid touching the other with even the smallest part of our tense, angry skin.

I thought about what normal people usually do in situations like this. They probably turn their backs to each other and try to sleep. The next morning, everything looks different. The next morning, everyone has work to do and they don't feel like arguing anymore, at least not with the same passion. The next morning, the argument is magically buried in that mysterious place where we always put all our arguments. I'm not saying that they disappear, I'm not that naïve, but I know the lid can be closed relatively easily. Sometimes, you need to sit on it, like you do with luggage, but nevertheless, if you've supplied yourself with a half-decent suitcase for packing arguments, you'll be able to close it.

My husband is silent on his side of the bed, hoping, I guess, that I'll stop there. Actually, it could be so simple: all he needs to do is turn towards me and give me a hug. Still, this is something he never does in situations like this. His only contribution is stubborn silence. Meanwhile, his silence has always been such an inspiration to me ever since the first time I wanted him to kiss me, instead of just sitting there, not saying a word.

"I know how this will end," I say. "Sooner or later we'll make up and act as if we never said any of those things."

He's lying silently in the darkness, but I know he's listening to me.

"That's one of the biggest deceptions in a marriage," I continue. "At some point, people get tired of arguing and say to themselves: 'All right, it's over now, we can make up, with or without sex, it doesn't matter, I just want it to be over because I don't have the will or the energy to continue with this.' At some point, we realize all those stories in marriage manuals and the marriage advice in women's magazines are pure nonsense, and that all these things are very different in real life. None of the arguments have ever turned into a constructive conversation. Nor will this one. At one point, the two of us will begin to act like we've made up."

It was strange. I was still there, in the argument, the pillow was still wet from my tears, I could still feel the left side of my body being pierced by a wire fence of hatred, which erupts out of nowhere and then very quickly vanishes who knows where; but at the same time, it was as if I was looking in from the outside. I've learned in all these years the way it usually begins, the paths it takes, and how it ends. We resembled two well-rehearsed actors modestly celebrating the 300th showing of a small chamber play. The set sometimes changes, the décor is falling apart, so new set pieces are dragged in, they broke a few tea sets during the years, and as time passed, they took the liberty of changing the original text. They even got it into their heads that they knew more about what the characters should say than the writer himself! They were able to start from the middle, the end, go backwards, if needed. They could have done the play in a large, luxurious theatre or on the stage of a small, provincial movie theatre. It was all the same to them. They've surpassed the required amount of applause a long time ago. Everything after that is a plus. Such were our arguments.

I wanted to ask him where he thinks the hate goes after we fall asleep, or decide to end an argument, but I knew I wouldn't get an answer. At least not one that would allow me to expand my theory. My husband doesn't believe hate is an integral part of love.

Nevertheless, I wanted to bring this out into the open, and so I said:

"Since you're so stubborn, both you and I know that at some point I'm going to turn around and hug you. In fact, that's what you're waiting for. So we can then finally go to sleep."

Instead of an answer, I got some sort of subdued, obscure groan, something like disapproval, like a sigh of a man pretending to be worn out.

I could lay my hand on his chest now. I wouldn't find it hard. Or unpleasant. I could pretend I'm upset because we fought. But I'm not. I'm completely indifferent, because, at this point, a fight doesn't mean anything, nor does a kiss. That's what I'm talking about. At a certain point, it all becomes equally unimportant and almost the same. The only thing that changes is the position of the hands on the clock.

Maybe he was able to follow my train of thought, or not, besides, it wasn't really that important. As I already said, none of it was important. That's why he was given only bits and pieces, with the opportunity of putting them together as he sees fit.

"It's all love, I guess," I said to him from my wet pillow.

This is when he got the courage to slowly turn his head towards me, for the first time.

"Do you know what love is?" I asked the pillow next to me.

He didn't say anything, of course. He had no intention of falling into the trap.

"More than anything, love is the fear of loneliness. That's love. People added all the other things simply to shield themselves from banality."

He had already turned towards me, and was looking at me in the dark. I could hear his breathing and feel the barbed wire fence become softer and silkier. Soon, I'll be able to walk through it without any injuries.

"I'm afraid of loneliness. You're afraid of loneliness. We're all afraid."

His breath was nearing mine, and hate sensed it was time to go back into its dwelling place. Without dinner, but still rewarded with a long walk.

My hand moved towards his face and he was there. And that was plenty, much more than the possibility of him not being there at all.

SIXTEEN

Extension cord, contact lens solution, deodorant, soap, doormat. This is a list of things I need to buy today.

In this city, children like killing cats. I don't think it was always like this, at least not when I was a child. Something changed. Either the children, the cats, or me. This is a city of angry children. If they could, they would smash all the car windshields, puncture all the car tires, scribble dirty words on all the walls, urinate in front of everyone's door, and spit after everyone they pass on the street. Then, they would go and slowly choke some cat. Or sic two or three stray dogs on her that are just as pathetic and angry as they are.

It was summer already and we were helplessly sitting on the terrace watching children, barely three feet tall, run around the building, with wild looks on their faces, as they let out terrifying screams. Some were carrying sharp sticks. Others were grabbing rocks along the way. Still others were relying on their ability to kick hard. I could see them turning into people who beat their children, right before my eyes, and then these children beating other children and the anger building to a point I don't dare think about. It was unbearable, no matter where we sat. Inside, it was humid. On the terrace, we had to watch them. There was no point in trying to read, because every few minutes, we would hear a beastly cry coming from the mouth of a child whose arrival into this world was once greeted with joy by everyone.

This is how we happened to escape into the mountains, to a house that belonged to our friends.

Everything seemed different there. The air was fresh, the grass was truly green, the birds and flies were considerate and discreet, the nights were quiet and the days were long.

"Remember how the summers never seemed to end when we were kids?" said my husband, with his feet up on the fence, wrapping a sweater around his shoulders.

I knew exactly what he was talking about. Time had

begun to flow outrageously fast. Birthdays ran one right into the other, seasons changed before you got a chance to finish a book, weekends came around at the blink of an eye, and then another and another… and everything in-between was the same.

Here, the days were suddenly long again. Our mornings began by slowly opening the wooden shutters, looking into the hills, observing the sky and the occasional clouds, followed by making casual, interesting plans for breakfast, going for a walk, and dicing vegetables for lunch. Then, we might take a nap, and there was no reason why we couldn't go for another walk. By late afternoon, we would feel like the day started at least three days ago because we had already done so many things.

In the evenings, we played cards and drank beer. This was how we spent our days and then, on the last evening of our stay, we saw this forty-year-old woman with a pleasant singing voice on TV, when our friend, our considerably drunk friend suddenly said:

"What is she doing on TV at her age?"

I could have let this go, of course. This was only one of those things he says when he's drunk. But for some reason, I felt the need to confront him.

"And why wouldn't she be on TV?"

"Because she's old."

His wife sat up on the sofa and grabbed her cigarettes. You could feel an argument coming on.

"What are you trying to say," I asked, "that only young and very attractive people should be on TV?"

He was pouring himself another beer and you could tell he had no intention of backing down. Besides, he was quickly approaching his fortieth birthday and we were supposed to interpret all this as fear, but for some reason, we didn't want to.

"It's unbecoming," he said, as if he wanted to stir things up even more. "They're taping her music video from a helicopter so that we won't see her wrinkles."

"What about Pavarotti?" my husband stepped in.

"It's different with Pavarotti," said our friend. "He's a man."

It was obvious he was trying to provoke us. I made one final attempt:

"Come on, you don't really think that, you just want to annoy us."

"Oh yes, he definitely does!" suddenly his wife jumped in. "In his opinion, all women who are not anorexic, or are over eighteen, should be subjected to senicide."

"Don't take it personally. I'm only talking about the singers."

"Listen," I said. "You know very well that's ridiculous."

"It's not ridiculous. Flip through the channels and tell me what you see. Young, fresh meat. That's what the viewers want!"

His wife's lips curved slightly downward. It was obvious her disappointment wasn't anything new, but at the same time, there was something in her eyes that frightened me. There were already too many disappointed people in the world. I didn't want to add to someone's pile of crushed illusions. But, he wouldn't stop:

"Here, take a good look and tell me if I'm wrong! The place is dominated by young, firm, slim, new, desirable… old women in their forties have no business being there. Like it or not, it's true!"

Great. We've finally come to the hard facts, I thought to myself. I could have told him he should never talk that way in front of his wife, but he already knew that. I could have told him the people in that room were no longer truly young, or really firm, or as desirable as they once were, but he already knew that too. I could have engaged in a long and boring analysis on desirability as an altogether personal and not always rational feeling, but I wouldn't be telling him anything he didn't already know. Something else was making him say these things, something impossible to defeat. Or, at least difficult to defeat. And on that night, none of us had the strength for hard, grueling verbal battles. I could have told him that he probably feels the same way we all do, but that perhaps he wants to deal with the inevitable as soon as possible.

My mother came to mind. And how, as the years passed, she became increasingly angry with the whole world. Angry with time. Angry with pharmacies, store prices, mendacious plumbers, small dress sizes in store windows; angry with the tiny print on the labels of her favorite cosmetics, angry with the dark spots on her hands and face, the blood pressure monitor, the television program that offered nothing, absolutely nothing, to amuse her; angry with her own anger, which she then tried to pass off as great concern for the world around her, which was recklessly and stubbornly falling apart.

A few destroyed civilizations came to mind. I wanted to say that maybe they were ruined for this exact reason, because some angry, powerful old man tried to prove that the problem lies in the depravity of the world and not him.

The next morning, we all acted as if nothing happened. Except that she came to breakfast in her nightgown. I guess being neat and pretty wasn't that important to her anymore.

They waved to us from the terrace as we got into our car and left for the city where children kill cats.

I wanted to tell my husband that it all came down to the same thing, but we were driving down a winding road and I refrained from talking about it. It was all the same and anywhere we go, sooner or later, there will be death and cruelty and destruction. The only difference is in the scenery.

SEVENTEEN

We would go down to the lake at night and swim in the dark, after everyone had already gone, leaving behind only the calm, warm water, the music from the nearby floats and the stars.

I would lie on my back and float on the water, imagining I was floating through space. As my ears filled with water, I would hear only distant, undefined humming which, in my imagination, easily became the humming sound of outer space. I would leave only a small part of my face above water, just enough to watch the stars above me.

The universe was rocking me. The stars moved closer and then withdrew again. I was alone, terrified, and happy.

I felt like I was going to float like this forever because chances of someone finding me in such vast space were minimal. I wasn't even sure I really wanted to be found. I could sense eternity all around me.

Then I would swing my arms back a few times and the stars would start fluttering around me.

I thought of Edgar. What is he doing right now? He probably just got back from work and is fixing dinner. He has turned on the TV and is waiting for his baseball game to start. Soon, he'll sit on the sofa and eat his dinner while watching television. For a moment, he might think about how it's not good that he's spending another evening alone, but the thought will quickly pass because the game will start to get interesting, and he'll surrender to forgetfulness. And fatigue. Edgar was very tired in the evening. I somehow knew that.

Later, when darkness spreads over Baltimore as well, he will go up on the roof to watch the stars. He'll open a can of beer and think about how the billboards are bothering him. They gleam and flicker and get in the way of him watching the night sky. He'll remember the way he waved at the street camera the other day. He'll start feeling sorry for himself, and think, "Loneliness can really drive a person to do pathetic things." Was that the phone or was he just imagining it? He'll realize he was just imagining it, as usual. No one ever calls him at this hour. He'll start wishing he had a telescope so that he can see what the other people were doing in their apartments. Then he'll tell himself that that would make him even sadder because he would get to see people sitting around with their friends and talking. Arguing. Making love. Eating dinner. Ironing. But not alone.

I knew Edgar was well aware there were many other lonely people besides him, but he also knew this realization is of no comfort to them.

"Hey!"

I saw my thoughts glance off the stars and move towards Baltimore.

"Hey, Edgar! I'm talking to you!"

Edgar holds his breath. Turns the television down. Leaves the beer can on the table. Gets up and looks out the window.

"I'm not outside, Edgar. But I could be, very soon, if you like. It's only a few hours by plane."

By now he's standing in the middle of the room, completely baffled, with an almost frightened expression on his face.

He looks about and then in a low, very low voice, says:

"Where are you?"

"There, right above you. I'm floating among the stars."

"So, that's it. I've gone crazy?"

"If I'm crazy, then so are you."

"I have to tell you, I've never been a religious man. And I wouldn't want to start now."

"This has nothing to do with God, Edgar. This is purely science. Stars, pheromones, the speed of light, planet curvature - things like that. I can't really explain it to you, but I feel like we're on the trail of something great."

"How can I be sure you're really you?" asks Edgar, more relaxed now and back on the sofa again, with the can of beer in his hand.

"Ask me something. Test me."

"All right," says Edgar, trying to think of a question. "What is the greatest passion of all?"

"Fear!"

"You're quick. Very good. Here's something more difficult: what is the cruelest thing of all?"

"That's easy. Beauty."

"Hmm. Very, very good. I have just one more question for you. Name an art form in which there is no skepticism."

"Edgar, everyone knows that. It's music."

The last thing I saw was how the very last trace of innocence disappeared from Edgar's face. He seemed to have opened his mouth to say something else, but that was when my husband swam over to me, touched my leg in the water, and the line with Edgar was cut off. I looked up again, but I no longer knew which of the stars bounced my thoughts towards him. It all disappeared in a blink of an eye. I couldn't get it back. At least not tonight.

EIGHTEEN

I've been trying to find a parking space for an hour now. I tried all the usual methods: discreetly waiting for someone to leave their spot, circling around the block, picturing in my mind, with all my might, a nice empty parking space waiting for me just around the corner. Casually driving around as if I had no intention of stopping, looking at the buildings instead of the sidewalk in an attempt to throw off my bad luck that morning; in other words, I tried everything. But, there wasn't a single parking space within a radius of a few kilometers. It was just one of those days.

I stopped and lit a cigarette, and then turned on the radio. Joe Cocker was singing. This is good, I thought to myself. Why am I even in a hurry to leave this spot? It's late summer, there are people all around me, I'm shielded by the very pleasant shade of a tall linden tree, and I'm not in the way of the other drivers, who are free to continue on their way. Who needs a parking space?

And then the phone rang.

"What are you doing?" my mother asked in a solemn voice.

There's been friction between us for the last few days, since our last Sunday dinner together. Sunday dinners with our parents remind us that we're failures and that we didn't meet their expectations.

I made my voice sound cold, which I will undoubtedly feel guilty about later on:

"I'm trying to find a parking space. Nothing special."

"I wanted to see if you were all right," my mother continued in that same voice, as if she were on her deathbed.

I guess I was supposed to ask why her voice sounded like that, but I didn't feel like it. I've asked that question too many times already.

"I'm fine, of course."

"Last night I had horrible nightmares," said my mother. "And I became terribly worried about you."

I could have replied to this in several different ways.

I could have asked my mother what the nightmares were about. But, then I would probably have to listen to how I was faced with another deadly situation.

I could have told my mother that every dream, in which I'm devoured by something or killed or run over on a crosswalk, actually represents her aggression towards me. But, then she would probably start crying.

I could have gently said I was fine and avoided asking about her dream out of consideration for her feelings, which we don't want to stir up again.

I could have uttered one of those sentences that solve every problem by putting the blame on the weather. Mentioned the storm that roared all through the previous night and told my mother we were all a little groggy due to the sudden change in weather. I could have backed this up by mentioning some newspaper article and saying that such heat waves had never hit London, and that the North Pole is going to melt quickly if this continues. And that the continental climate of our city is slowly becoming tropical. All this has to affect our dreams in some way, right?

I could have snapped at her and told her it was silly of her to call me on my cell and tell me that she once again had a bad dream about me.

I could have asked her: "Are you saying that something bad or tragic is going to happen to me soon? Is that your message?" And then she would probably start shouting: "Oh, no, no, no.... I just wanted to see if everything was all right, I woke up and my heart was pounding so hard I just had to call you...." But, then I would be faced with the heart palpitations, which I couldn't or shouldn't ignore, if I wanted to call myself a daughter. I would have to ask why her heart was pounding, and then she would say it had been like that for days. No, she wouldn't mention the argument, but you could read between the lines that she had been in really bad health ever since the day we had the argument, during the damn Sunday dinner, and that she didn't want to worry me, but since I already asked, she just didn't know how to hide it. Even though she really wanted to keep this from me because the last thing she wanted was to worry me.

I'm putting my make-up on in the rear-view mirror and imagining one of the possible replies:

I'm sorry, Mother, that today I didn't meet with anything that could match your supreme talent for the tragic, your flair for the melodramatics. The world might never see the superior manner in which you would wrap your pale and righteous face in black, in keeping with deep mourning. Mourning attire before which everyone in the room would have no other choice but to fall silent at, and perhaps let out an uncontrollable sob or two. This would be one of those performances that leave the audience nailed to their seats, even after the curtain goes down. They would feel it inappropriate to stand up and applaud. They wouldn't know whether to throw flowers at your feet or go home in deep and solemn silence. Sometimes I feel guilty for robbing you of the role of a lifetime. Because I want to live a few more meaningless years or decades, you can't fulfill your potential. That's really sad. If only I were doing something worthwhile with my life, it would be understandable that I should be alive. But this way… here I am, sitting in my car in the middle of the street, incapable of even finding a parking space. And, what's worse, I don't care. I care so little that I might not even go to work today, and simply go back home and watch cartoons. And for this, you're missing out on your career.

How do her fears unfold? Are they complete stories, overflowing with details, infusions, deep wounds, death-rattles, coffins, telegrams of condolence, gladiola arrangements, and tears, or just terrifying flashing images that freeze her body, somewhere between horror and the thing she calls love? What does she feel when I come back from a trip, when the plane lands, when I leave the hospital, when, for the hundredth time, I challenge the prophetic power of her dreams? Is there at least a tiny bit of awakened disappointment or is all this called relief and joy?

My mother told me, on numerous occasions, that she has been terribly afraid for my life since the day I was born. Once long ago, she asked her father if this was normal and, according to her, he said that fear was a normal phenomenon, which always accompanies parenthood. And so my mother was also given formal permission to continue with her fears, because, of course, she didn't tell her father that she was going to do so to the very end, mine or hers, with a force which, in my opinion, surpasses rational parental concern. Still, I know nothing about parenthood, so I'm not the one to judge. However, since this concerns my life, I am so bold as to make judgments about her fear.

Of course, I could always turn to the cruelest option: I could ask her if she maybe wanted us to quickly and simply confirm her ability to predict horrific events. For example, I could drive my car into the first wall. Or even better: I could take my hands off the steering wheel and run off a bridge into a swollen river.

My mother would sit, surrounded by her friends, and between sobs, tell them about the horrible nightmare she had the night before, and how she knew, just knew, something terrible would happen. And no one would be able to dispute this. So, if she was right about something that serious and fatal, this could only mean that she was right about all those other things, which were far below this event in the hierarchy of fate.

I finished putting on my make-up. It was time to finish the conversation as well.

"I'm fine," I said to my mother, like someone who was in the middle of heavy city traffic and couldn't talk a minute longer.

"Well then," she said, disappointed, "good-bye."

The light on my phone was blaring for another full six seconds, as if asking me if I wanted to call her back.

I do, I thought to myself. Of course I do. But that wasn't what was really expected of me.

"I've almost finished my novel," I said.

Summer was nearing its end and I was once again sitting in my chair, after taking a break for several weeks.

There was nothing new, really, except that now she had short hair. But, I felt like I needed to give her some encouragement.

"That's good. I remember the first time you were here you mentioned some sort of writer's block. Are you happy with what you've written?"

Writer's block!? What an expression! It reminded me of the phrases used in bad literary reviews.

"Well, that's a hard question. I don't really know how I feel about what I've written until the novel is completed. And even then, I'm not sure it's any good. Sometimes I think it's good and other times, it seems completely mundane. I don't think it's spectacular, but it's readable. For people who like this kind of psychological babble. I like it, and I always hope there's someone else out there who isn't squeamish about reading such things."

She laughed:

"And what would make it, as you say, spectacular?"

"Oh, if I knew that, I'd do it. This is something you know only after you read a spectacular novel. You simply recognize the real thing. I'm afraid there's no real recipe."

We could have gone on like that and used up my entire hour talking about literature, but somehow I didn't feel like she was the right person to talk to about this. I entrusted her with my stories before going on vacation and I asked her if she had read them over the summer. She told me she did and that she was a bit bothered by the fact that she knew the author. In any case, this was all I got out of her. I said:

"I, of course, gave you those stories because I wanted you to learn more about me through them."

"Or less," she added.

I liked this. Maybe she really did read them, I thought to myself.

I then told her about my most recent fight with my mother. About one more in a million fights.

"What is the recurring pattern in these arguments?" she asked.

"We already talked about that."

"It doesn't matter. There are so many things that need to be retold in order to put them in their right place."

"I guess the common denominator of all those arguments is the fact that I always take the bait. I always get angry. I always react like a hurt child."

"And what would be the mature reaction?"

"I don't know. If I did, I wouldn't be here. For a while, I thought the wisest thing to do was to keep from even participating in these conflicts. But that would only be a learned behavior. It wouldn't reflect my true need, if you know what I mean. Is it mature to adapt our behavior to the outside world, even though our genuine need for crying or getting angry or childish despair still remains the same? Is it mature to act like you're not afraid when you actually are? It can't be that the essence of maturity is simply well simulated calmness?"

"Of course that's not the point. It would be good if the calmness were genuine. How would you define, in one sentence, your constant clashes with your mother?"

"Guilt. I always feel guilty."

"For what?"

"For not being loyal enough. At least that's what she thinks. I'm not the kind of daughter she would want. A daughter who would talk to her every day about every detail of her life, and then give her a chance to offer her advice. A daughter who would then follow this advice, even if she doesn't agree with it."

"What is the opposite of this kind of loyalty?"

"Freedom, I guess."

"Do you feel free now?"

"No, not as long as she's alive."

"And what would constitute this freedom?"

"The first thing that comes to mind is the freedom to die. I can't die while she's alive. Don't get me wrong, I don't wish to die, but let's say I contract a deadly disease. You know what I'd be thinking about on my deathbed? I wouldn't get a chance to grieve over my own life because of the guilt I would be feeling for doing this to my mother. That's exactly what it would be like. Me dying would be like doing something unforgivable to my mother! But, when it comes to, let's say, my husband, I wouldn't feel that way. In relation to him, I would just feel sad for leaving him. But, no guilt."

"What trait does your husband possess, which makes him different and unlike your mother?"

"I think he genuinely loves himself, in a healthy and normal way, whatever that means. If I were to die, he would without a doubt be sad and grieve for a while, but he would manage to get back on his feet and continue with his life. And that's good to know. It's not at all pleasant to know that you're dragging someone else with you to your grave. When I drown, everyone else should stay safely on the surface, until their time comes. That would be real freedom!"

"Who do you think gives us permission to love or not love ourselves?"

"Why, our parents, right?"

"And what if we don't get this from our parents? What then?"

"Well, I don't know. If we don't get this from our parents, then we simply don't have it."

"Do you know that only a person who genuinely loves himself can truly love someone else, or really belong to someone else?"

"Are you saying that I can't genuinely love another person?"

"I want to remind you of a conversation we had some time ago about abandonment, which results from fear of being abandoned."

If she had thought of those coloring pencils and drawings at that moment, if she had asked me to draw love, the way

I saw it, then and there, I would have probably drawn a knife entering a deep and aching wound. It would have been a cheap, symbolically very primitive drawing, but still, damn it, a very precise presentation of what I was feeling. Somehow, I knew this couldn't possibly be good. This was not what love was supposed to look like, I guess. My father's lips pressed tightly together came to mind. And that I wasn't really familiar with his eyes because he wore tinted glasses all his life. I remembered the displeased look on my mother's face, greeting me as I approach her on the street. She doesn't talk about it anymore, but I know there are many things she would like to change about me. Does being mature mean you should simply overlook their angry, dissatisfied, critical faces? I remembered the way my husband always came home with a pure, cheerful smile on his face, and I thought of my fear of being taken to some unfamiliar regions of boredom due to the sameness and certainty of this smile. Why would I be bored only when I'm in a place where that knife isn't turned every day in a wound inflicted long ago? Maybe I really can't feel genuine love for anyone. What a devastating thought. All I wanted to do was write a novel; meanwhile I've come to the realization that I don't know how to love. I thought maybe I got more than I bargained for. But, there was no going back.

I asked her:

"So, what do I do now? What comes after we reveal the people

who are to blame for our defects, and the list of complaints against our parents and everyone else who did us wrong? Is there anything after that? Or are we left only with our awareness of the devastating revelation, banished from the world of those who know how to love?"

"You have the capacity to make up for this. You can call it your inner nurturing parent or, simply, a gradual awakening of love towards yourself."

I was sad and tired, and I didn't believe this could be corrected, ever. I asked her:

"Do you really believe it is possible?"

"Yes, I do. It's a process. It takes time. In some cases, it's a never-ending process, a job that is never completely done, but it can bring results. This is something we need to work on from now on."

There's nothing riskier than drawing a big conclusion - both in novels and psychotherapy. This is why I didn't say anything significant to her at the end of that session. Nor did she. We made an appointment for the following Wednesday, at 6:00 p.m., which will probably be another beautiful September day, just like this one. Somehow, autumn always fits in better with my idea of beauty than spring. Maybe it's because my mother preferred orange and brown tones, or simply because I think I look better in a raincoat than a tight top.

NINETEEN

It was raining in Baltimore, of course. The morning was grey and foggy, the air was sticky from the humidity and everyone was in a big rush to get somewhere, with their heads down, carefully carrying their umbrellas. In a few minutes, Edgar would show up at the bus stop, where I was standing, waiting for him.

A woman was adjusting her hood as she walked by.

Another woman was about to step in a puddle of water, but when she suddenly swerved to avoid it, she ran into a curly-haired man who was walking his dog, and got tangled up in the leash. They smiled at each other and continued on their way.

A man wearing a grey raincoat inserted a coin into a vending box, raised the lid, and took out the morning paper.

Two streetlights were still on, even though it was already daylight.

Everything looked familiar and ordinary from this side, as if I'd already stood at this bus stop, with a pretzel in my hand, numerous times.

I'm going to tell Edgar that, ultimately, loneliness is a matter of choice.

I'll admit to Edgar that I had to pay for everything I'm now bringing to him.

I'll submit to Edgar this little report on me.

I'll share my pretzel with him.

I'll turn my computer off, get up, and go home to make tomato soup.

I'll tell Edgar this was always possible in the past, but that this morning, it no longer is.

I won't even wait for him to show up. I'll turn my computer off before he comes. That's easy enough.

I'll admit to him that, in some way, I'd like to be there now, in front of my computer, and that I was just imagining all this, like many times before.

I'll drive really fast over the bridge with my eyes closed and count to ten. Maybe even fifteen.

I'll tell Edgar I decided to visit him the day I finally drove my car across the entire bridge without opening my eyes once. I'll tell him the fear I felt on that day was now behind me.

I'll turn the stove on and open the refrigerator, while I think about the last sentence.

I'll run the car off the bridge.

I'll throw myself into Edgar's arms.

When my husband comes in, I'll shout for him to close the door because of the draft.

The next day, there will be a small article in all the newspapers about the bizarre accident.

No one will ever find out why I left, where I went, or what happened to me.

Some will try to find clues in my first and last novel, and they will search for me in Baltimore, in vain.

I'll observe the soaring air bubbles and think about Virginia Woolf.

I'll tell my husband how I hate books with morbid endings.

I'll get up from the table and give him a kiss.

A huge neon sign will light up with the words HAPPY ENDING.

Before going to bed, I'll have a cup of cocoa with plenty of sugar.

I'll flip through the channels a little.

I'll go to sleep.

ABOUT THE AUTHOR

Jelena Lengold was born in 1959 Kruševac, Yugoslavia (now Serbia). She is an accomplished storyteller who has published eleven books since 1982, including six poetry collections, four short story collections, and a novel, Baltimore. Her work has been translated into several languages, published in multiple anthologies, and is critically acclaimed across Europe.

Lengold has received multiple awards for her books. Her short story collection The Fairground Magician has won the Biljana Jovanović, Žensko pero, and Zlatni Hit liber awards, as well as the European Union Prize for Literature. Her poetry books Images from the Life of a Kapellmeister and A Well of Heavy Words have received the Đura Jakšić Award and the Jefimijin vez Award, respectively.

Lengold worked as a journalist and editor for the culture desk of Radio Belgrade for ten years before becoming a project coordinator in the Conflict Theory program of the Nansenskolen Humanistic Academy in Lillehammer, Norway. Since 2011, she has worked and lived in Belgrade, Serbia, as a freelance journalist and writer.

OTHER BOOKS BY JELENA LENGOLD

1. ***RASPAD BOTANIKE (Decomposition of the Botany)***, poetry, Pegaz, 1982.

2. ***VRETENO (The Spindle)***, poetry, Nolit, 1984.

3. ***PODNEBLJE MAKA (The Climate of the Poppy)***, poetry, Nolit, 1986.

4. ***PROLAZAK ANĐELA (Angels Passing By)***, poetry, Nolit, 1989.

5. ***SLIČICE IZ ŽIVOTA KAPELMAJSTORA (Images From the Life of a Kapellmeister)***, poetry, Prosveta, 1991.

6. ***POKISLI LAVOVI (Rain-soaked Lions)***, stories, Srpska književna zadruga, Savremenik edition, 1994.

7. ***LIFT (Lift)***, stories, Stubovi kulture, Minut edition, 1999.

8. ***BALTIMOR (Baltimore)***, a novel, Stubovi kulture, Peščanik edition, 2003;

Second edition published by Arhipelag, Zlatno runo edition, 2011.

9. ***VAŠARSKI MAĐIONIČAR (The Fairground Magician)***, stories, Arhipelag, Zlatno runo edition, 2008.

10. ***PRETESTERIŠI ME (Saw Me Up)***, selected stories, Arhipelag, Zlatno runo edition, 2009.

11. ***BUNAR TEŠKIH REČI (A Well of Heavy Words)***, poetry, Arhipelag, Element edition, 2011.

12. U TRI KOD KANDINSKOG (At Three at Kandinsky), stories, Arhipelag, Zlatno runo edition, 2013.

AWARDS

For the book of poems ***Images From the Life of a Kapellmeister*** she received the **Đura Jakšić Award**.

For the collection of stories ***The Fairground Magician*** she received the following awards: **Biljana Jovanović**, **Žensko pero**, **Zlatni Hit liber**, as well as the **European Union Prize for Literature**.

For the book of poems ***A Well of Heavy Words*** she received the **Jefimijin vez Award**.

www.ingramcontent.com/pod-product-compliance
Lightning Source LLC
Chambersburg PA
CBHW070632310726
48982CB00001B/257

9781613430521